The Travels of Oggy

Ann Lawrence has lived most of her life in the place where
she was born – Tring in Hertfordshire. She says that her
interest in wild life started when she was a child, and this
interest was reinforced after working for the British Trust
for Ornithology. She is passionate about music and cricket,
and she enjoys bicycling, ambling round ancient monuments,
and looking at pictures.

Ann Lawrence
The Travels of Oggy

text illustrations by Hans Helweg

Piccolo Books London and Sydney

First published 1973 by Victor Gollancz Ltd
This Piccolo edition published 1976 by Pan Books Ltd,
Cavaye Place, London SW10 9PG
6th printing 1980

Text © Ann Lawrence 1973
Illustrations © Hans Helweg 1973
ISBN 0 330 24640 2
Printed and bound in Great Britain by
Richard Clay (The Chaucer Press) Ltd, Bungay, Suffolk

Contents

1 Oggy Meets the Family 7

2 Oggy Loses the Family 15

3 Oggy Sets Out 22

4 Oggy and the Cat 32

5 The Rat and the Canal 40

6 The Bridge 49

7 Oggy Meets Hodge 63

8 The Crow Explains About Bad Ends 74

9 The Question of Badgers Again 85

10 Badger at Home 93

11 Badger's Story 102

12 The Whole World 109

13 'See You Next Spring' 119

For my Father

1 Oggy Meets the Family

Oggy was a hedgehog, who lived in a hole under a tree stump, at the end of a garden, behind a house, in a part of London called Belsize Park. He had not always lived there; once he had lived with his mother and some brothers and sisters on Hampstead Heath, but almost the only thing he could remember from that time was his mother saying:

'Remember, Hampstead Heath is not the Whole World.'

Oggy certainly remembered that Hampstead Heath was not the Whole World, though the information was not a great deal of use to him, as he had no idea of what his mother meant by 'the Whole World', and his memory of what Hampstead Heath actually *was* faded quickly from his mind, until all that remained was a vague recollection of a great deal of grass and some brothers and sisters. The brothers and sisters were rather hazy too: they had not come to Belsize Park but Oggy had no idea why they had not come. It did not strike him as very strange. He knew nothing about family life, and for all he knew it was quite normal for brothers and sisters to disappear; he did not think it was anything for him to worry about.

It is only a short journey from Hampstead Heath to Belsize Park if you go by car or bus; it is not all that far if you have to walk, but it was a very long way for Oggy and his mother, snuffing their way from garden to garden, until they came to one that smelt right. They even had to cross several roads, and the second thing that Oggy remembered his mother saying was:

'Remember, never roll up on roads – run!'

That was difficult to remember, because of course whenever a hedgehog is frightened, he automatically rolls up into a ball, and that is enough to discourage most of the things that might hurt him: nobody likes prickles in their nose, after all. But since prickles do not worry car wheels, the only way for a hedgehog to be safe on a road is to look both ways and hurry across, like anyone else. A lot of hedgehogs forget, or never learn, that the one place where they must never roll up, no matter how frightened they are, is on a road, and so a lot of hedgehogs get squashed, but Oggy and his mother always remembered.

They had not lived in the Belsize Park garden for very long before Oggy's mother disappeared one night and never returned, leaving Oggy the sole occupant of the hole under the stump. He was lonely and anxious at first, for in all his life until then he had never been completely alone, but he was so busy just keeping himself alive, that the memory of his mother soon became as distant as the memory of his brothers and sisters. However, he never forgot what she had told him.

The hole was just the right size for a full-grown hedgehog, and Oggy was now nearly full-grown. The garden in which he lived and other gardens around it provided him with plenty of food – slugs, insects and scraps that people threw out on their compost heaps – so that Oggy had only to follow his nose to find his dinner.

Because he followed his nose all the time, and mostly after dark, he did not actually see much of his surroundings for quite a long time; in fact, being short-sighted, he relied very little on his eyes, anyway. He knew where the house was, because he had once gone right up to it, and had sniffed his way to the back door. It smelt promising, but since there was no way of getting in to investigate those interesting foody smells, he did not trouble himself over it again. He did not,

therefore, know anything about the people who lived in the house. In fact he knew nothing at all about any people. He knew something about houses and cars. He had once found a bottle of milk on a doorstep, and accidentally pushing it over while investigating it, he had been most impressed by the taste of its contents, but he had never associated any of these things with human beings. He was not the least bit interested in human beings: they were large and noisy and went about on two legs.

One evening Oggy's nose caught a smell it had never before encountered; it was definitely foreign to the garden, and Oggy simply had to find out all about it. There was no trail to this smell, it was just there, in the middle of the lawn, and it belonged to something as strange as itself. Looking at the thing, Oggy would have said that it was a stone, but his nose told him that it might be something to eat. Biting it, Oggy would have said it was a stone, but his tongue told him that it *was* something to eat – something sticky and very sweet. He thought it over for a minute: the thing was a stone to his eyes, his paws and his teeth, but to his nose and his tongue it was something very good to eat. On the whole he trusted his nose and tongue more than his eyes and paws, so he decided that his teeth would have to do the best they could, and he tackled

9

the thing again. This time a bit of the thing broke off in his mouth, and dissolved very sweetly and stickily on his tongue. He did not need any more convincing – it was certainly something to eat, and so he settled down to eat it right away.

Hedgehogs are not the quietest of animals. They snuffle very loudly when they are sniffing out their food, and they are rather noisy eaters too. It might be imagined from this that they are dreadfully ill-mannered creatures, and it may be that some of them are, but there is this much excuse for them: they cannot sit down comfortably to their dinner and take their time over it, because they have to eat everything they catch right where they catch it, and then hurry off after the next course, so there is bound to be rather more bolting and gulping than you would see at the best dinner tables.

Oggy had made a great deal of noise, even for a hedgehog, while he was searching for the strange smell, and when he had found the-stone-that-wasn't-a-stone, he made even more noise tasting it and trying to eat it. Indeed he made so much noise – such a sucking and sniffing and scrunching – that it was heard by the people in the house.

Oggy's nose was full of the smell of his find, and his ears were full of the noise he was making eating it, so that he did not smell or hear the man, until he stood right over him. As soon as he sensed that he was no longer alone on the lawn, Oggy rolled up, but not as tidily as usual, because he would not drop his sweet stone; or perhaps it was so stuck to him that he could not let it go if he had wanted to. He tucked his nose in as well as he could and waited, expecting the man to go away soon.

To his amazement and horror the man did not go away; instead he bent down and rolled Oggy over. Oggy nearly stopped breathing, but he stayed tightly rolled up, being quite sure that since he was not on a road, nothing could possibly happen to him as long as he stayed rolled up. He was very put out, therefore, when he felt himself being carefully picked up, and he was not at all happy to realise that he was being carried into the house. Although he had his head tucked in and his eyes shut, Oggy knew that he was no longer out doors, and that there was a bright light somewhere near. He was placed on a hard floor, and then nothing happened for a little while except some unfamiliar noises, which he could not hear properly, because he was so intent on staying rolled up.

The muffled noises stopped. Oggy heard someone put something on the floor near him, and there was silence. Oggy waited and waited; still he could hear nothing, but a new smell was tickling his nostrils – a smell that particularly interested him. For a minute he completely forgot about his 'stone'. Ever since he had broken that milk bottle and drunk the contents, he had been on the look-out for more of the stuff, but though he had made quite a nuisance of himself by going round all the back doors in the neighbourhood and knocking the milk bottles over, he had never again encountered a full one. Now here he was in a strange and possibly dangerous place, with the smell of milk very close to his nose. A little while longer he waited, torn between caution and greed, and then, since there was still no sound to alarm him, he unrolled and looked around for the milk.

There it was, a saucerful of it right in front of him, but there too were four enormous figures sitting round him on the floor. He drew his head in a little, as if he were going to curl up again, and thought: People; Very Large People. His head shrank in a little more, but then he thought: they haven't done anything threatening yet, and one can always curl up again if they do make any threatening movements, and there's the milk ... Oggy's tiny black eyes glanced round quickly: two very enormous and two only gigantic people doing nothing (they were a man, a woman and their two children, a boy and a girl). Oggy decided to chance it and moved forward towards the milk.

It was only when he moved that he remembered that he still had the thing from the garden stuck to his paws. He stopped again: which should he have first, the thing or the milk? It was not really a very difficult choice, for he had been hugging the thing so tightly, that it looked as if the only way he could get it off his paws was by eating it off. With one eye on the saucer of milk, to see that it did not go away, he set about the sticky stone again.

There was a movement and a murmur as the people leaned forward to see what Oggy was doing. One of them (it was the boy) put his head down to the floor to see better.

'It's a lollipop! The hedgehog's got a green lollipop!' he exclaimed and sat up laughing. It was a very sudden, loud noise, and rather close to Oggy's ear. He stopped scrunching, ready to roll up again, but nothing happened, and so he went on eating the lollipop. The people had started talking quietly, but Oggy decided that it was not an unfriendly sound and ignored it.

When he had finished the sweet, Oggy looked round, and then he looked up, which was something he rarely did, since he was usually following his nose and watching the ground. He inspected the people more thoroughly than he had before: they looked all right, they smelt all right. On the whole he thought they seemed quite harmless. He turned to the milk and drank it quickly. As he did so, it occurred to him that these people were rather better than harmless, for he was almost certain that *they* had provided the milk. He had never bothered to join his ideas about things together before, but now they started to join up of their own accord. Where had he found milk before? Outside a house. Where was this milk? Inside a house. What else was inside the house? People.

Milk – doorstep – house; house – people – milk. Oggy thought he would like to know these people better.

The last of the milk disappeared and Oggy considered what he might do next. He was not the least bit hungry now, nor the least bit afraid, but he *was* curious. Generally he took life very much as it came: Hampstead Heath then Belsize Park; brothers and sisters then no brothers and sisters; mother then no mother – he just plodded and snuffled on through everything. But so many things had happened so quickly tonight, he had been obliged to do so much thinking, that he could not just take it all for granted. An unfamiliar feeling stirred inside him. It was a bit like being hungry, and a bit like being frightened. Oggy did not recognize it, but in fact it was his Spirit of Adventure.

Ignoring the people now, Oggy set off round the room (it

was the kitchen) on a tour of inspection, snuffing at all the promising, tasty smells he had found at the back door. His good opinion of the people and their house increased; this was definitely a good place to know, a place which could offer even more than milk and lollipops, if he came here often enough. When he had seen and smelt all he could in the kitchen, he looked the people over once more, and then made for the back door, which had been left open.

He plopped clumsily over the doorstep and wandered off into the dark garden again, with the firm intention of returning – completely ignoring several slug trails which crossed his path on the way back to the stump.

2 Oggy Loses the Family

Oggy's guess about the house and the people was right. It *was* a good place to know, the people *were* the providers of milk, and the enticing smells that he had found in the kitchen and around the back door did occasionally materialize as a plate of food, left for him by the doorstep. It was not the grown-ups who were responsible for the regular supply of milk that Oggy now received, and the other occasional titbits, for they were inclined to believe that it was cats that ate the food and drank the milk.

'The hedgehog couldn't possibly be living here,' they said.

The boy was not very interested after a while, and forgot about Oggy, but the girl continued to think about him, and knew for certain that it was the hedgehog, because she always remembered to leave something outside for him, and sometimes, if she waited at the window for a while, she saw him come for his supper.

'How do you know it's the same hedgehog?' said her brother, and all she could say was:

'It must be, because he knows where to come.'

After his visit to the house, Oggy had become fascinated by it and the people. Although he never went into the house again, he often looked up at the lighted windows and saw the people moving about inside. There were french windows at the back of the house, and once when he saw a light behind them, but no movement in the room, Oggy crept up to the glass and peered in. He could not make much sense of what he saw, since he knew nothing at all about how people live, but he thought it was all rather pretty.

Before the night when he had met the people in the house, he had thought of the stump as his home, and the garden he took for granted as his hunting ground. Now he began to feel that the house and the people were somehow 'his' as well. 'What are My People doing?' he would say to himself, if there was some sign of unusual activity in the house: 'That cat's got no business to be in Our Garden,' he would think crossly, when the next door neighbour's cat disturbed his hunting – and often he sat on the lawn looking up at the bright windows, thinking: 'how smart Our House looks.' The garden, the house, the people and himself all belonged together as far as Oggy was concerned, and the little girl was his friend (for he had seen that it was always she who put his saucer of milk by the doorstep every evening at dusk).

Now and then there would be no lights in the windows, no noise or movement in the house, and no milk by the door for a night or two. Oggy had no idea what happened at these times, and the question did not trouble him. It was tiresome to miss his milk, but on the other hand the little girl nearly always put something extra with the saucer when it next appeared, as if to make up for nights she had missed – usually it was a sweet or a biscuit, which in Oggy's opinion almost made it worth going without the milk once in a while.

Because of this Oggy was not at first worried when he shuffled out of his hole under the stump one evening and saw the house in darkness, even though it did occur to him that it looked somehow different. On the next night also the house was dark and silent. Two nights without milk, thought Oggy sniffing a little irritably, that should be worth something special tomorrow night, and he went off to find his supper, wondering what the treat might be – one of the hard sticky things? Or one of the crumbly things? Perhaps it would be both; a toffee and a chocolate biscuit, he decided, that would be very acceptable – two nights was a bit too much after all.

When he found the house still dark and milkless on the third night, Oggy began to feel uneasy, and on the fourth he noticed other things, which were somehow strange. The place had a sad, blank look about it; there were no toys in the garden, no milk bottles at the back door, and most sinister of all, there were no smells. Oggy snuffled hopefully round the house, but only the faintest memory of those lovely, nourishing smells lingered round the back door. The smells of the people and their dog and cat had gone too.

When Oggy came to the french windows, he stood up on his hind legs and leaned against the glass, peering into the room as he had done before. It was quite dark inside, and Oggy could not remember now exactly what it had looked like last time, but he was sure something had happened to it: it seemed to be a different shape. It was all very peculiar. The house looked the same from the outside, but it was different inside, and it smelt cold and unfriendly. Oggy did not like it at all.

He was still standing there, staring through the french windows, when he heard a voice right beside him.

'Gone!' it said.

Oggy dropped down on to all fours again and looked round. A mouse was sitting on an upturned flower pot, not a foot away from him, washing her face as if her life depended on it. Oggy stared at her.

'What?' he said. The mouse stopped abruptly and stared back; after a moment she said in a clear, precise voice:

'The people who lived in this house have gone away,' and scratched her ear vigorously with her hind foot.

'They've gone away before,' Oggy remarked, thinking of the other times when the house had been dark, 'not usually for such a long time though,' he added. The mouse sniffed at him.

'It's different this time,' she said, 'this time they've taken everything with them. Didn't you see?' She nodded towards the french windows.

'It looked as if the shape of it had changed inside – there were lumpy things before,' said Oggy slowly, trying hard to remember how the room had changed.

'That's right,' said the mouse impatiently, 'they've taken the furniture; the house is empty.'

'What's furniture?' Oggy asked suspiciously. He thought the mouse was being altogether too clever and superior in her manner.

'Those "lumpy things" of course, stupid!' said the mouse witheringly. 'Chairs, tables, cupboards, drawers – things they sat on and put things on. Don't you know *anything*?'

'How do *you* know so much?' Oggy demanded, all his prickles twitching with annoyance.

'I live inside in the winter, and come and go as I please,' she said smugly.

'All right, clever, when are they coming back?' Oggy snapped.

'Ah!' said the mouse, pointing a forepaw at him in a bossy, hectoring manner that he did not like at all. 'Ah-*ha*! That's *it*. They *aren't* coming back. Not *ever*, hedgehog, so there's an end to milk and sweets and biscuits for *you*. I know all about that – oh yes – but now you'll have to find your own living, like an honest animal.'

The mouse sat back looking triumphant. Oggy's little black eyes fixed on her angrily.

'You nasty, jealous, sneaking . . .' Oggy snorted furiously, and the mouse started to squeak with shrill laughter.

'No use looking at me like that,' she squealed. 'It's not my fault they've gone.'

'How do you know they've gone for good?' Oggy shouted.

'I heard them talking about it,' said the mouse, jumping up. 'Over and over again the children were saying that they were going away and not coming back. Dancing around, singing—' the mouse capered about on the flower pot, chanting – '"We're going to the Country."'

'What's that?' said Oggy irritably. The mouse stopped prancing about and waved her front paws vaguely.

'A long way away,' she said airily.

'You don't know,' Oggy said, squinting at her intently. The mouse looked a little put out, and she could not think of anything to say immediately. Oggy had an idea.

'So, they've gone to the Country at last, have they?' he continued knowingly. 'They've intended to for a long time, you know,' he nodded thoughtfully. 'They'll be expecting me to follow in my own time, though they might have warned me.'

'All right, then, where is the Country? And *what* is it?' said the mouse in a strained voice, her whiskers twitching madly.

'Oh I couldn't explain it to *you*,' said Oggy grandly. 'Poor little mouse. You wouldn't understand, and it's much too far for you to go.' He shook his head kindly.

The mouse stared at him for a second, and then with a squeal of rage she flounced off the flower pot, and disappeared into the darkness.

Oggy trundled into the garden chuckling to himself. That was a good joke; that shut her up, and what a good idea too. He'd follow his people to the Country – a real inspiration, that. As the night wore on, however, Oggy's cheerful mood faded. He had been so pleased with himself about annoying the mouse, that he had forgotten that he knew no more about the Country than she did. Not only did he not know *where* it was, he did not even know *what* it was, so there was little chance of his going to it. All the same, he would have to go somewhere, for if he stayed here, living in his hole under the stump, the mouse would be sure to know. She would guess the truth, and he would look a terrible fool.

Oggy waited another day, but when the night fell there was still no sign of life in the house. He hunted gloomily through the night. It was not the milk or the sweets that he minded about, he told himself, though of course he would miss all that. It was something else, not quite so clear in his mind as the idea of food, but just as important these days. He did not belong to anything any more, and belonging had been nice. It was the not belonging that he minded.

As he was making his way back to his hole towards dawn, he met another mouse.

'Hallo,' it said. 'Are you the hedgehog that lives under the stump?'

'Yes,' said Oggy cautiously. 'Why?'

'Oh nothing,' said the mouse. 'Only I thought you'd gone to the Country.' And it scuttled away sniggering.

Well, that's it, thought Oggy, as he settled down to sleep. I shall have to start as soon as night falls. I can't stay here any longer.

But where was he to go?

3 Oggy Sets Out

Oggy left the garden in Belsize Park early in the evening, with only the vaguest idea of what he was going to do. His plan, such as it was, was to get well away from his old home, and then start asking everyone he met about the Country. Once he had found the Country, he could start asking after his people.

The more Oggy thought it over, the more simple and reasonable it seemed, and he began to get quite confident. That strange feeling, which had come to him first in the kitchen of the house – that adventurous, exploring spirit, which was a bit like being frightened, came back to him. His dull life of food, sleep and very little thought had been spoilt for him when he met the family in the house, and his interests had been stretched to take in his people. Now here he was setting off on An Adventure – which just shows, Oggy thought, how careful you ought to be about getting interested in things.

Oggy had been so anxious to start that he had set out when it was barely dusk and there were still a few birds around. Useful, thought Oggy, birds go everywhere and gossip terribly; one of them is bound to know about the Country. The difficulty was to find a bird on the ground at a time when most of them were flying home to roost. Just as it was becoming really dark, when Oggy had given up all hope of finding one, he was crossing a piece of untidy open ground where some houses had recently been pulled down. Suddenly a flutter of grey caught his eye. He thought at first it was a piece of paper, but then he saw that it was a pigeon pecking around in the rubbish.

'Hey, Pigeon!' he called, running towards the bird. 'I want to go to the Country . . .'

'Travel broadens the mind,' said the pigeon vaguely, and flew off.

'Well,' said Oggy crossly to himself, 'that's very encouraging I must say!' And he stumped away across the rubble towards the next lot of gardens. But unknown to Oggy, someone else had overheard his short conversation with the pigeon. Two pointed ears twitched with interest, and four black feet followed when Oggy moved on.

For some time Oggy wandered among the gardens of Hampstead, looking for someone who could tell him about the Country, but in vain. Now and then the four black feet went off on business of their own, but all through the night they were seldom far behind him.

At last Oggy came to a garden which boasted a small lily pond, from which came the sound of a frog singing. Well, thought Oggy, even if he can't help me, at least it would be someone to pass the time o' night with, and so he made his way to the edge of the pond.

The frog was sitting on a lily leaf, right in the middle of the pond, his head thrown back, his eyes closed and his throat swelling with a slow, rasping song of great sadness, all about the terrible misfortunes of his life. All very well, thought Oggy, sitting down on the edge of the pond to wait politely for the frog to finish his song, but I must say he looks comfortable enough at the moment. It was indeed a beautiful garden and a luxurious lily pond. When it became apparent to Oggy that the frog was quite capable of going on like that without a break all night, he snorted and coughed gently to attract the singer's attention. When that failed, he stood up

and said, 'Excuse me –' several times, very politely. Finally he shouted in the loudest voice he had:

'Mr Frog!'

The frog shut his mouth, opened his eyes and looked a little puzzled.

'Excuse me, Mr Frog,' Oggy began, 'but—'

'Were you listenin' to me singin'?' the frog inquired hoarsely.

'Oh – yes,' said Oggy.

'Ah,' said the frog. 'Then you was expressin' your appreciation.'

'Well – it was very – well – very *moving*,' said Oggy in some embarrassment, for he had thought it was awful.

'Ah, you couldn't know the 'alf of it,' said the frog, his eyes closing once again. 'It moves *you*, but it breaks my 'eart.'

'I'm sorry about that,' said Oggy, squinting doubtfully at the frog.

'Sorry?' croaked the frog tragically. ' 'Oo arst you to be sorry? You don't know what sorry is – an easylivin' 'edge'og like you – traipsin' round bein' moved, an' sayin' you're sorry. Life o' Riley that is!'

'I beg your pardon,' said Oggy stiffly, 'but I only stopped to ask if you knew anything about the Country. I've no wish to . . .'

'Country,' cried the frog. 'What would I know about the Country? Me what's never even bin to 'Ampstead 'Eath. 'Emmed in all me life by brick walls, I bin,' he groaned. 'Never a day out, never a breff o' clean air. I never even bin to Soufend or Battersea Fun Fair when I was a nipper. I was the youngest of five 'undred, as never knoo farver or muvver . . .'

Tears rolled down the frog's face. He threw back his head, closed his eyes, and launched once more into the long, sad song of his life. Oggy snorted in disgust, and turned away from the pond. As he trundled away, he said very distinctly:

'Some people should be grateful for what they've got, or go and find something better!'

Of course the frog did not hear; he hardly ever heard anything that anyone else said, but Oggy felt better for saying it, and a pair of sharp eyes glittered with amusement in the shadows.

By now Oggy sensed that it was going on towards daybreak, and still he had no idea about how to find the Country.

Giving up all hopes of learning anything useful that night, he decided that he would make his way to Hampstead Heath, and start again from there the next night. It was a long time since he and his mother had come from there, so that his recollections of the Heath and the journey were very vague now, but after a few minutes of sniffing the ground and sniffing the air and thinking hard, he thought he could feel the way. Pointing himself in more or less the right direction, he set off briskly – four black feet coming along behind him.

To reach the Heath, Oggy had to cross a large road, and though it was a long time since he had last come that way, he could still hear his mother's voice saying:

'Remember, never roll up on roads – run!'

Oggy stood on the edge of the road, looked carefully along it in both directions, and then started to trot sedately across. He was somewhere near the middle, when a great roaring burst on his ears – huge lights rushed towards him. For a moment he dithered in the middle of the road, wanting so much to roll up, but then he ran as fast as he could for the far side, and the car swept past him. He tumbled breathless and trembling into the grass beyond the footpath, and lay there sorting himself out, while four black feet crossed the road behind him and a fine set of whiskers twitched very thoughtfully...

Oggy had just about recovered his breath, and was about to carry on, when a smooth, dangerous voice suddenly spoke right by his ear:

'*What* an interesting hedgehog!' it said. 'I really thought you'd had it just now.'

Oggy, still a little shaken from his last fright, rolled up instantly. To his horror, two black forepaws immediately unrolled him again, and he looked up into a pointed brown face, with very bright eyes and large, pointed ears.

'There's no point in doing that, you see,' said the brown animal. 'I could have eaten you any time tonight, if I'd wanted to, but I don't fancy hedgepig just now. In fact, I'm not hungry at all, I'm interested.'

'Who are you?' Oggy asked weakly.

'I'm Fox,' said the animal grinning, 'and sometimes I rather do fancy pork.' Oggy shrank and tried to roll up again.

'No, no, you know that's no good. It's not a very intelligent thing to do, hedgehog, I had thought better of you. Besides, I want to talk to you, and it's hardly polite to roll up when you're being spoken to.'

Fox prodded Oggy in the tummy with one paw.

'Let me go then,' said Oggy, pulling himself together a little.

'Ah, a sturdy hedgehog,' said the fox. He sat down, cocked his head on one side, and looked Oggy over, while that unhappy animal waited stolidly to hear what he had to say.

'A London hedgehog who wants to know about the Country?' Fox mused. 'A hedgehog who crosses roads carefully and doesn't roll up in front of cars. An intelligent hedgehog, perhaps.'

'Well? What about it?' said Oggy growing impatient.

'A *bold* hedgehog!' Fox exclaimed, grinning again. 'Tell me, urchin, why do you want to know about the Country?' He poked at Oggy again with a black forepaw. Oggy told Fox briefly about the people, and how they went away, and how he thought he would like to follow them to the Country.

'Well, well. An adventurous and enterprising hedgehog!

I hardly thought there was anything left in the world that could surprise me, but an adventurous urchin is certainly something new to me,' cried the fox. 'And what about crossing the road? How did you learn to defy your instinct like that?'

'My mother taught me,' said Oggy.

'What a very wise urchin, to pay attention to parental instruction to such good effect,' Fox said admiringly. 'But you don't really know much else about the world, do you?'

'I know that Hampstead Heath isn't the whole of it,' said Oggy, who was beginning to tire of the fox's heavily patronizing tone, and did not wish to be too much underestimated.

'No, indeed,' said Fox, rather baffled by the remark. 'Neither is London the Whole World, if it comes to that.'

'Can *you* tell me about the Country?' Oggy asked him.

'Naturally,' said the fox. 'I lived in it for years, before I came to Hampstead.'

'What's it like, then?' Oggy demanded. 'And where is it?'

Fox thought for a minute or two.

'You know where we are now?' he said at length. 'Hampstead Heath.' Oggy nodded. A picture of the Heath came into his mind: a large patch of grass with some trees.

'Well, you know that London goes all round it?' Fox went on. Oggy nodded again, and a ring of houses sprouted up thickly round the patch of grass in his mental picture.

'Right then, the Country is very much like Hampstead Heath – lots of trees and grass and whatnot – and it goes all round London, like London goes all round the Heath.'

Grass and trees grew up round the houses in Oggy's imagination, and stretched endlessly in all directions.

'Well, well, well,' said Oggy. 'And is *that* the Whole World?'

'That's right,' said Fox, which just goes to show that people do not always know as much as they think they do.

'Well, well, well,' said Oggy again, and then something rather awkward occurred to him. '*All* round London?' he said anxiously, 'in *all* directions?'

'That's right,' said Fox again, pleased with himself for making the explanation so clear to this simple creature.

'A lot of help that is!' Oggy exclaimed. 'They might have gone off in any direction into all that Country, so I still haven't the slightest idea of which way to go.'

Fox looked distinctly offended. He frowned and curled his lip.

'I've told you what the Country's like and where you can find it,' he said sourly, 'and now it's up to you to manage for yourself. Just walk in a straight line in any direction from here, and eventually you're bound to find some Country. I suggest you do just that, and forget about these people. You don't stand the slightest chance of finding those particular ones again, so if you must have people, though I can't imagine why, you'll have to take up with some new ones. There's always too many of the creatures, wherever you go, so that should be no problem.'

Oggy did not care for the look of Fox's frown. It seemed to him that if he annoyed this fine gentleman, he might decide that he was no longer interested in talking to hedgehogs, however enterprising, but might suddenly feel more like eating them. He therefore thanked the fox humbly and profusely for his help.

'Not at all,' said Fox, gracious and kindly once more. 'I'm only too glad to encourage enterprise in the young. There is one more thing you might add to your store of wisdom, though.' He grinned and reached out a paw towards Oggy, who started to feel nervous again. 'Don't roll up for foxes, and look out for Badger, too. You'd better learn to climb trees, I should think.'

The fox turned to leave him, but Oggy called anxiously:

'Whatever are badgers?'

'Badger is an old country gentleman, with whom I once shared lodgings. He's always very partial to hedgehog,' Fox said over his shoulder, and he trotted away into the dawn mist, grinning to himself.

Oh dear! thought Oggy as he scuttled around looking for somewhere to lie-up safely for the day. Travelling in the Country sounds much more difficult and dangerous than I thought.

4 Oggy and the Cat

Oggy's encounter with Fox had given him plenty to think about, and he stayed where he was, on the edge of Hampstead Heath, for several nights, thinking about it. It was obvious to him now that he was most unlikely to find his people, which meant that his main reason for going to the Country had disappeared for a start. Also Fox had said that the Country was very much like Hampstead Heath. Oggy had hoped that it would be something quite new and different, but if it was just the same as something he already knew, what was the point of going? That disposed of his second reason for wanting to go to the Country.

All the same, it was a great anti-climax to have decided on such an adventurous plan and then to do nothing about it. The feeling he had enjoyed, of being the bold, resourceful urchin, dwindled. He was just a dull, stodgy hedgepig after all. But Fox had called him enterprising. Fox had not eaten him because he thought him intelligent – sturdy. Oggy scratched himself vigorously. A sturdy, intelligent hedgehog would go to the Country just for the sake of the adventure. Never mind about people or whether it was different – it was *there*, it was an adventure, and so he would go!

'What about foxes?' said a voice in his head. 'What about badgers?' Oggy looked thoughtfully at the nearest tree. Fox must have been joking about tree climbing. Still, it would not hurt to try it some time, just in case.

'Just in case of what?' said the voice. Well, just in case of meeting a fox who is not interested in conversation, Oggy told himself, just in case of badgers. 'How would *you* recognize a badger?' said the voice, and there Oggy had to stop listening to it, because he had not the slightest idea of what a badger might look like. It seemed to him, on reflection, quite likely that the first badger he recognized would be the one that made a meal of him.

'Still want to go to the Country?' the voice insisted. Oggy could not shut it out. For a while the bold enterprising hedgehog and the dull, cautious hedgehog argued inside him, but at last his adventurous self won. His intelligence and resourcefulness would certainly see him through, he told the voice, as it had when he crossed the road, as it had in his meeting with Fox.

The last thing to be decided was which way he should go. Now that he had given up the idea of following his people, it did not matter which direction he took, if there was indeed Country all round London, as the fox had said. By sniffing and asking around a bit, Oggy discovered that he was on the north-west side of Hampstead Heath. If I go south or east, he thought, I shall have to go across the Heath, and then across a bit of London after that. But if I go north or west, I only have to go through a bit of London: north or west, which shall it be? Eventually he pointed himself north-westwards and set off.

During the first night of his travels, he made his way cautiously from garden to garden, as he had when coming from Belsize Park, only crossing roads when they lay right across his line of progress. Late in the night, he came to a long row of gardens which ran in exactly the right direction and provided him with an easy route for some time. They were all about the same width, and of more or less the same shape and layout. It was a little boring, perhaps, but it gave Oggy a convenient measure of his progress. Moreover, he did not have to waste time sniffing and feeling out his route, and he was able to pick up all the food he needed, without going far out of his way.

He had traversed some twenty gardens in this row, and was just squeezing himself under a fence into the twenty-first, when he saw something moving stealthily in front of him. He stopped, and then drew back a little, so that only his head poked out from under the fence, and strained his eyes and nose to make out what it might be. The creature kept to the shadows, but Oggy could see that it was not as big as a fox. As he had no reason to believe that there were badgers in London, he shuffled into the garden as quietly as he could, and followed the moving shadow. Suddenly it stopped, and in that moment Oggy caught its scent. It was a large, black cat.

Oggy was naturally relieved, but also rather cross at having been so cautious. It had shown him how nervous all this business of foxes and badgers had made him, and he felt a bit silly. He did not think that adventurous hedgehogs ought to be nervous at all, let alone nervous of cats. He watched the cat resentfully. She had evidently been stalking something, and now she was about to pounce on her prey, tensing and wriggling forward to make her jump. It occurred to Oggy that he could get his own back on the cat for frightening him, and have a bit of fun at the same time, by creeping up on the cat and startling her, just before she sprang on the mouse. Holding his breath, he scuttled up to the cat, trying to imitate her movements.

Oggy was so amused by the cat's stealthy wriggling, and his own imitation of it, that he was nearly bursting with laughter. When he was quite close to her his amusement broke out in a terrific snort and a sort of sniffling giggle. The cat jumped right off the ground in surprise, twisting round to face Oggy as she landed, her back arched and her tail fluffed up like a bottle brush. She glared at him fiercely.

'A hedgehog!' she hissed furiously. 'A nasty, snuffling, slug-witted hedgehog!'

She advanced a step towards him, but Oggy only ducked his head and grinned, knowing that she would not attack him. He need only curl up, and she would never risk her tender nose and paws on his prickles. The cat knew it too. She lay down and stared at him.

'I just don't know how you manage to catch the revolting creepy-crawlies *you* live on,' she continued nastily. 'I should think even a beetle would hear your disgusting snorting a mile off.'

Oggy sniggered a little.

'What's the matter with you?' he said. 'What's all the fuss about?'

'I suppose a person might well make a fuss, when some stupid oaf has just lost a nice fat mouse for her,' the cat snapped back.

Oggy tried to look very serious and apologetic.

35

'Good gracious,' he said quickly, 'I had no idea, really. I mean, I always thought you moggies were so well fed and all that. I didn't realize you had to hunt for your dinner just like anyone else. I wouldn't dream of depriving a poor, starving cat . . .'

Oggy's voice faded out as the cat squatted down in front of him and fluffed herself up to an immense size, her eyes narrowed to slits.

'Look here, hedgehog,' she said in a fat voice, 'let's just get one or two things straight.'

Oggy's little black eyes gazed back at her innocently. She was the sleekest cat he had ever seen, and she had probably never been hungry in her life, not even a bit peckish, let alone starving.

'In the first place,' said the cat smoothly, 'I prefer not to be called a "moggy". I understand that term to signify any old common-or-garden cat, and *I* happen to be half Persian, which puts me in rather a different class of animal, as even you, Creature, must realize. In the second place, I have an exceptionally good home, with people who appreciate what it is to associate with a very superior feline, and provide me with every luxury a cat could ask for: fish, liver, cream . . .'

'What!' cried Oggy, making a face which was supposed to express righteous indignation. 'You mean you don't *need* to eat mice? I call that downright wicked! Blood sport, that's all it is – harassing us poor wild things just for your own pleasure. Aristocracy! Luxury! What is it?' he demanded, recalling the aggrieved tones of the frog, and producing a creditable imitation of them. 'It's Grinding the Faces of the Poor!'

He concluded on such a note of triumphant self-righteousness, that the cat completely lost her composure for a moment.

'Impertinent vermin!' she spat. 'If you weren't wearing that filthy pin-cushion coat I'd show you some blood sport!'

'Ah!' said Oggy smugly. 'If . . .'

The cat recovered herself quickly. She was determined not to lose her temper and give Oggy the satisfaction of seeing that he had made her look silly. To show her complete indifference to him, she sat up, turned away slightly and began to wash her front paws.

'As to the matter of aristocracy, a poor ignorant creature like you wouldn't understand what a strain that kind of life is,' she said over her shoulder. 'You couldn't realize, of course, that if I didn't go hunting, I should get hopelessly out of condition, with all that food and comfort. You simply don't understand about living with humans. It's such a bore having to entertain them all the time – having to sit around and be fussed over. One simply has to escape from it all sometimes and go back to the simple life of one's ancestors.'

She spread her claws daintily and nibbled the fur between them, her eyes closed, her face smooth and round with indifference. Oggy might have been an old broom-head lying on the grass for all the interest she took in him.

'Huh! I know about people, too,' Oggy said scornfully. 'I was a great friend of a very nice family. A *friend*, mind you – I always had my own home. *I* was never a pampered house pet.'

'I'm sure you weren't,' said the cat, staring at him roundly. 'I can't imagine any human allowing you over the doorstep.'

'That's all you know,' said Oggy. 'I used to go into the house, and they gave me milk and biscuits and sweets – oh, all sorts of things. They thought a Great Deal of me.'

It did not sound as grand as Oggy would have liked, even when he had exaggerated his one visit to the kitchen into a regular event. He had not thought that *his* people were boring at all; he had been very excited by his one experience of the inside of a house, and now the cat was making him feel that he had been a great simpleton to be so impressed. The cat gave him a superior smile.

37

'If they thought so much of you, whyever are you wandering around now, like some squalid tramp?' she said.

'They've gone to the Country, and I am following in my own time,' said Oggy, going back to his old story. 'I like travelling,' he added.

'They've gone to the Country, leaving their dear little friend to follow in his own time? That doesn't sound very likely, even if he does like travelling,' said the cat, her eyes narrowed again. 'Where have they gone?'

'North-west,' said Oggy quickly, since that was the direction he had chosen.

'But you don't know *exactly* where they've gone, do you? You haven't got their new address, have you?'

'I shall ask after them,' Oggy assured her confidently. 'Someone will be bound to know them. There are four of them – a man, a woman, a boy and a girl.'

'Good heavens,' the cat cried in tones of great amusement. 'You really are the most wonderfully ignorant creature! Don't you know that there are thousands of families just like that? Look at all these houses: there are four people just like yours in every one of them, I should think.'

'They've got a dog and a cat,' said Oggy uncertainly.

'*All* of them have dogs and cats,' the cat said scornfully. 'They all have cars, too, so don't tell me that, and television sets, and refrigerators – all the same, see? Same people, same house, same garden. Same outside, same inside. Why, sometimes when I go in at night, I wonder if I'm in the right house!'

Oggy knew so little about the inside of a house, that most of this was incomprehensible to him, but he had had enough of the cat and her airs, and thought it was time he got going again.

'Do you ever wonder if you're the right cat?' he grunted, and turned away to shamble across the garden.

The cat nearly burst with rage, and her attempt at aristocratic calm finally broke down.

'You miserable, dirty flea-bag!' she yelled after him.

Oggy was rather hurt. References to fleas always upset him, because people just did not understand. Maybe he did have fleas, but he was perfectly clean. *All* hedgehogs have fleas, he told himself, lots of fleas – lots of *clean* fleas.

'Fish-face!' he shouted back. 'Fatso-catso!'

But they were rather feeble insults, as he knew. Perhaps he *was* just a common, ignorant animal, he thought gloomily, as he went on his way.

5 The Rat and the Canal

During the following night, Oggy found himself in an area which seemed to be arranged in the most awkward way possible. All the streets seemed to lie across his path; there were too many open spaces to cross, and there were fences and walls everywhere. Altogether it was so confusing that he completely lost his bearings several times, and wandered out of the way he had fixed for himself. At last, after several hours of anxious sniffing and scrambling (in which he did not have much time to find food, because it was a full-time job finding the way), Oggy crept under a board fence, to find before him a narrow strip of open ground and then a strip of water. Some tall buildings loomed darker against the dark sky on the other side.

Up to that time the only stretches of water, larger than a puddle, that Oggy had ever seen, were garden ponds, and so he assumed that this too must be a pond, although a very odd one. He puzzled over what kind of garden it could be. The buildings on the other side of the water, which he supposed to be the house to which it belonged, were not very far away, so it was not a very long garden, but since he could see no end to the pond in either direction, it must be tremendously wide.

He was very relieved to discover, after a good sniff round, that he did not have to cross the water. In fact he would be going in just about the right direction, if he followed the path that went alongside it. After all the confusion of his night's travelling up to then, it was nice to find such a clear, convenient route, and Oggy hoped it would continue for a good distance. He thought too that it would be interesting to see more of this peculiar pond.

An hour later Oggy was very puzzled indeed. Still he had not come to the end of the pond, still the path continued to run alongside it in the right direction. On the other side of the water he saw that there were sometimes houses, and sometimes open spaces. Where there were buildings, they were sometimes close to the water, and sometimes further away. He was clearly not in a garden belonging to one particular house, and this was no sort of pond he had ever seen before, but what exactly it was, he could not imagine. However, it was very useful, and that was all that really mattered.

Suddenly he saw ahead something which at first he thought

must be the end of the pond, but as he approached the place, he realized that it was only something jutting out from the bank. As he came nearer, he saw that it was not even part of the bank, for it was moving very gently, swaying and bobbing a little. The way it moved reminded Oggy of the water lily on the pond, where he had seen the frog. It must be floating on the water, he thought, but whatever can it be? It looks as big as a tree trunk – bigger.

Oggy approached the thing cautiously, and going right to the edge of the bank, he sniffed the nearest end of it. He thought it smelt like wood, all right, but not really like a tree. He started to walk along it, inspecting it closely. He had walked more than half the length of the thing when, to his great surprise, he came to a tiny window. A window – and at the same moment he caught a distinctly kitcheny smell!

'Goodness! It's some kind of house!' he exclaimed aloud. 'A floating house!'

'Not quite a house, matey,' said a voice from somewhere above his head. Oggy looked up and saw a rat sitting on top of the thing.

'It's a boat,' the rat continued, jumping down beside Oggy. 'A canal boat. Otherwise known as a narrow boat or a barge.'

'Well I never,' said Oggy wonderingly. 'And why has it got windows? *Do* people live in it, like in a house?'

'They do,' said the rat. 'Though that ain't the principal use of it. It's for carrying stuff up and down on the canal – coal, iron, timber – stuff like that.'

'Canal?' said Oggy inquiringly. It was the second time the rat had used the word, and Oggy had never heard it before.

'This here water is the canal,' the rat explained. 'It's not like a river. A river's natural, a canal is man-made – like a big ditch.'

Oggy was completely lost. He understood that this bit of

water was called the Canal, but all this about ditches and rivers might as well have been Double Dutch, for all he understood of it.

'I thought it was a kind of pond,' he said shyly, expecting to be told once again that he was ignorant.

The rat laughed and shook his head.

'A pond!' he shouted. 'Some pond, eh? Hundred mile or more long. Some pond!' But he did not tell Oggy he was ignorant.

'I'm sorry, but I've only seen water in ponds. I don't know anything about canals, or ditches, or rivers,' Oggy said.

'No reason to be sorry,' said the rat, still grinning. 'No reason why you should know anything about any kind of waterways, if you've never been near 'em before. Now I've lived on the canal boats all my life, so you'd expect me to know something about them.'

Oggy was encouraged to find someone who did not appear to think him altogether stupid, for his meeting with the cat the night before, and losing his way several times tonight, had rather shaken his self-confidence.

'I should like to know about the canal,' he said.

'You would?' said the rat, sounding quite surprised. 'I never met a land animal before that cared two hoots about the water.'

He stared at Oggy.

'Well you see,' said Oggy, 'I don't know anything about it, so I'd like to find out about it. I don't know much about anything, you see, and I'd like to know about something,' he finished despondently.

'If you're going to find out about everything you don't know about, you're going to be blooming busy,' said the rat, grinning. He stroked his whiskers. 'Well now, where shall we start? Do you know anything at all about any kind of running water?'

Oggy thought hard. 'I've seen water running down gutters after it's been raining.'

'Gutters,' the rat repeated. 'Yes, well – you could say a ditch is a kind of deep gutter, and a canal is a big ditch. And the canals go all over the country, like the roads.'

'Roads go all over the Country!' Oggy exclaimed. 'I thought there were only roads in London. What are they for in the Country?'

'Same as they are in London, of course,' said the rat laughing. 'For cars and things to go on; the canals are for boats to go on.'

'But why?' said Oggy, feeling that he was being terribly stupid.

'To get from town to town. Canals and roads sort of join up all the towns, see?'

'Join up all the towns?' said Oggy. 'All what towns?'

'You know what towns are,' the rat said. 'Lots of houses and people – just like London. You're having me on, aren't you?'

'No, no,' said Oggy. 'I didn't know there were other places like London. Where are they?'

'All over the country,' said the rat. 'Not that they're all as big as London. Some are quite small places – but they're everywhere.'

Oggy remembered what Fox had told him. He saw again in his mind the patch of green for Hampstead Heath (which was not the Whole World), with the houses all round it for London (and that was not the Whole World either), and then the green Country stretching in all directions, all round London – green and empty.

'So there are towns all over the Country?' said Oggy, and little clumps of houses popped up here and there all over the green Country of his imagination.

'That's right,' said the rat. 'And canals and roads, remember.'

(Blue and black lines squiggled across the green from town to town.)

'Well, well,' said Oggy, 'Fox never told me that.'

'Very likely didn't know himself,' the rat said off-handedly.

The idea that there was anything that Fox did not know was entirely novel to Oggy, and would certainly have come as a surprise to Fox too.

'He said that London and the Country were the Whole World,' he murmured in amazement. 'Would London and the Country and the other towns be the Whole World?'

'Ah, I wouldn't care to say about the Whole World meself,' said the rat judiciously. 'It might be, and there again it might not. I don't know everything, do I?'

This, too, surprised Oggy, since everyone he had met lately had seemed quite sure that they did know everything.

'I thought everyone knew everything, except me,' he said.

'Well, how could they?' said the rat. 'If you believe everything folks tell you, you'll finish up in a right old mess.'

'That makes it a bit difficult to ask the way, though, doesn't it?' Oggy pointed out. 'If you can't believe what people say, I mean.'

'You do have to use a bit of common sense,' the rat agreed. 'But why would you be wanting to ask the way? *You* don't go far afield, surely?'

'I'm going to the Country, actually,' said Oggy, with assumed indifference.

'Blow me!' said the rat. 'I thought there was something about you that I couldn't make out. Fancy that, then!'

Oggy was pleased by the rat's surprise, but at the same time he remembered that he had not made much progress that night.

'I ought to get along,' he said, 'or I'll never get there.'

'You're walking all the way?' the rat exclaimed. Oggy nodded.

'That's what I call hard work,' said the rat shaking his head solemnly. 'Why don't you save your poor old feet and come along with us?'

Oggy stared at him.

'How?' he said blankly.

'On the boats, of course,' the rat said, laughing at him again. 'You just find yourself a corner where you can hide up during the day, and then when they tie up for the night, you go ashore, forage around for food and come back again before morning. Simple.'

Oggy was speechless with delight at the idea. The rat grinned at him, as he gasped some sort of thanks, but still it was a friendly grin. He did not seem to think Oggy particularly stupid.

'How long will it take to get to the Country?' Oggy asked, when he had recovered his wits a little.

'Be out of London by tomorrow night, easy,' the rat assured him. 'But you can stay with the boat as long as you like. We go all the way to Birmingham, and there's plenty of Country on the way, so you can get off anywhere you like the look of.'

He glanced up at the sky.

'It's getting on for dawn already,' he said. 'Better get aboard and settle down.'

The rat jumped nimbly on to the boat, but it was by no means so simple for Oggy to board. He was just not built for jumping nimbly, and he did not really trust the boat to keep quite still while he scrambled over the side. There was a very vivid picture in his mind of a hedgehog falling into the canal. At last, however, after running up and down the bank for a few minutes muttering 'ohdearohdearohdear', he plucked up

46

his courage and heaved himself over the side, where it was lowest.

'There's two boats,' said the rat, as he moved quietly along the barge. 'This one is the motor boat, and it tows the other one that doesn't have an engine – that's called the butty boat. I usually tuck myself away somewhere on the butty.'

The butty boat was tied up close alongside the motor boat, and the rat sprang across to it, as easily as he had come aboard from the bank. Oggy, deciding that he had cut rather an unheroic figure in his attempt to climb aboard, tried to copy him this time. Unfortunately his original caution had been well founded; while he did not actually fall into the water, the awkward little hop which he made from the side of the motor boat landed him in a heap in the bottom of the butty. That wasn't very heroic either, he thought crossly, the gallant hedgehog falls flat on his nose.

The boats were carrying timber, and the rat showed Oggy where he could creep under the wood to find a dry hole. When the rat had gone off to his own quarters, Oggy had a quick look round the boat. The hole the rat had found him was safe and dry, all right, but it was also rather draughty, and Oggy was used to a softer bed than bare planks. Within a few minutes, however, he found an old newspaper. This should do the trick, he thought, and dragged it back to his hole to make a bed. The movement of the boat felt very strange to him, as he shuffled round making himself comfortable. Don't suppose I shall sleep much, he thought, and fell asleep at once.

Some time later he woke with a start. There was a strange noise somewhere; he was being rocked about alarmingly. For a moment Oggy had no idea of what could be happening, but then he remembered that he was on the barge. They must have started: it must be day. Poking his nose out of his newspaper bed, he saw that there was light shining through the tiny gaps

47

between the planks. He was nearly frightened out of his wits by a loud thumping over his head, but he realized it must be someone walking on the timber.

'Noisy lot,' he muttered. He rolled up again and went back to sleep.

6 The Bridge

Oggy was woken by a great deal of scratching and scrabbling somewhere near at hand. He listened hard; the next thing he heard was someone calling his name, a thing which, as far as he could remember, no one but his mother had ever done.

'Oggy! Oggy! Where are you in there?' the voice called anxiously.

A good question, thought Oggy, as he shuffled round towards the voice. Where was he indeed, and why had he wrapped himself up in newspaper? And why was the ground so hard and yet so strangely unstable? Most curious of all, who in the world was interested enough in his existence to be calling his name?

'Are you coming out of there?' the voice demanded. 'There's no one around.'

Oggy sniffed. He was entirely surrounded by the smell of cut wood — wood, of course. The events of the previous night returned to him at once: the canal, the rat, the boat and lastly, thrillingly, the rat's promise that they would be in the Country tonight. He scrambled hastily out of his bed of newspaper and squeezed through the cracks in the timber, towards the rat's voice.

'I'm here, I'm coming,' he called anxiously, fearing that the rat might get tired of waiting and go off without him.

As he emerged from the stacked wood, Oggy blinked and ducked his head uncertainly. It was still too light, by his standards, to be out and about.

49

'It's all right,' said the rat, 'there's no one around. Gone to the pub, I expect.'

'Pub?' said Oggy. He no longer minded revealing his terrible ignorance to the rat.

'It's a house where people go to eat and drink. They don't do anything much else there, and they stay for hours,' the rat explained.

Oggy squinted around, but from the bottom of the butty boat he could see nothing of the world beyond the canal.

'Are we there?' he demanded.

'Where? Birmingham?' said the rat. 'Nowhere near it yet.'

'No, no, the Country,' Oggy said impatiently.

The rat grinned at him.

'What do you reckon?' he asked. 'What does it smell like?'

Oggy sniffed, and twitched his nose for a long time. It was not so much a question of what this place smelt like, as what it did not smell like. In fact, Oggy concluded, it did not really smell like anything he had known before. Even the smells he recognized, grass, water and leaves, were not somehow the same as the grass, water and leaf smells of London, and apart from these, everything that came to his nose was unfamiliar; every flutter of the air introduced him to a new language of scents. He sneezed, shook his head and then smiled slowly and happily at the rat.

'Well, it doesn't smell like London,' he said.

The rat said, 'I dug you out as early as possible, so that you could see a bit of the scenery, as well as sniff it. Thought we could go up on the bridge and have a look round.'

He turned and led the way to the edge of the boat and jumped on to the bank. Oggy dropped himself nervously over the side after him, heartily regretting that this waterborne life demanded so much agility. He soon discovered, however, that the acrobatics which he found so difficult to follow were not so much essentials of life afloat as personal characteristics

of the rat himself. He never climbed when he could jump, he never walked where he could run, and he would never run on the ground if he could possibly dance along a tightrope. Nor did it ever occur to him that any sensible animal who put his mind to it could not do the same. Oggy set his teeth and set off after the rat who was now running along the coping on the very edge of the bank. He had no time to look around just then, nor did he feel that it would be safe to pay attention to anything except where he was to put his feet next. All he gathered of his surroundings, as he shambled along at his best pace, was that the path by the canal was edged with grass and bounded by a hedge, instead of a fence, as in London. Suddenly the path divided, the right-hand branch passing under the bridge ahead, the left climbing a bank to go over it. To Oggy's horror, the rat took neither path, but leapt on to the end of a low wall between them, and started to prance along it.

'Hey!' shouted the despairing hedgehog. 'Where are you going?'

The rat returned to the end of the wall, and looked down at him in surprise.

'To the top of the bridge,' he said. 'Where else? You won't see a thing if you stay down there, you know. You've got to come up here on the parapet to look at the view.'

Oggy sighed. His eyesight was by no means keen, and he had never had any need to see anything further than a few yards away, so he was pretty certain that 'the view' would not mean very much to him. However, the rat was evidently anxious that he should see it, and he was sure that he had made a big enough fool of himself already, what with his ignorance and clumsiness, without adding to the bad impression by proving himself a coward as well. He started to climb laboriously on to the bridge and the rat turned to lead the way once more. Oggy lowered his head and shuffled up the slope of the parapet, taking care to see nothing but the brickwork at his feet, so that he would have barged right into the rat at the summit, had he not shouted:

'Woah there! You'll have us off, if you don't look what you're at.' Oggy stopped in his tracks and raised his head cautiously.

'Good,' said the rat, who was amused but kept a straight face all the same. 'Now take a look round, and tell me if it suits your tastes.'

Oggy looked round, and listened, and sniffed with deep concentration. As he had expected, the landscape was not very distinct to his near-sighted little eyes, but what he could see confirmed all the fox had said: it was indeed all incredibly green. It even smelt green, strongly, cleanly green: the smell of Hampstead Heath freed from the overlying smell of London. As far as his eyes could tell him, the Country *was* all grass and trees, with one or two houses dotted about in it, and it did stretch out in all directions all around him. He was not really able to compare it with Hampstead Heath since he had never seen that place, or any other, from such an elevated view-point. It was not, however, the discovery of these features of the Country that the fox had described which impressed him, but the things the fox had not told him about. The most impressive of these was the silence. Not a car or a voice was to be heard. Oggy stretched his ears, but all he heard was a rustle of wind in the trees near the bridge, and the tiny clucking noises of the water under the bridge. A blackbird flew along the hedge, officiously ordering everyone into bed, and one or two sleepy voices from other birds, out of sight, answered back. 'Shut up!' 'Go away!' 'Go to bed yourself . . .'

Oggy closed his eyes and beamed contentedly, as he soaked up the greenness and quietness. At last he turned to the rat.

'It's wonderful,' he said, shuffling round to face him, 'it's beautiful,' he declared, taking a step backwards, 'it's – help!'

Oggy's hind feet slipped on the edge of the parapet, the narrowness of which he had completely forgotten in his delight, and before he or the rat could do a thing, he fell back into the canal.

Oggy's first instinctive reaction to the disaster was of course to curl up, but as soon as he touched the water, and before it closed over him, he knew in a flash of inspiration that this was

another time when curling up was the worst thing to do. At once he uncurled again and tried to run, with the result that he started to swim straight down the middle of the canal.

The rat, watching from the bridge, was immensely relieved and equally surprised to see Oggy managing so well in the water, but his relief did not last long when he realized that the hedgehog was too confused by his accident to see that he would never reach the bank unless he turned.

'Turn right,' the rat shouted, running down the bridge. 'Turn in to the bank, turn right!'

Oggy's ears were full of the sound of water and his own gasping, and though he heard the rat shouting shrilly behind him, he did not hear the words. Suddenly through the gurgling confusion he heard a voice much nearer to him.

'This way,' it said firmly. 'Over here!'

He turned and floundered blindly towards the voice, and in seconds found himself among the reeds that grew by the canal bank. Puffing and blowing he scrambled out of the water and started to look round for the rat. He was surprised not to see him at once. Someone had directed him to the bank, and who could it be if not the rat?

'Well I never did!' said a voice from the reeds.

'I don't suppose you did ever,' said Oggy, rather peevishly, turning to peer at the reeds. 'What are you doing in . . .'

His voice tailed away nervously as he stared into a large, round, sleek face. The face smiled, showing a large number of white teeth. It was the smile and the teeth, particularly the teeth, that brought Oggy to his senses. Who was it who had called him to the bank? Why had Who called him? As the long dark body behind the face slipped out of the reeds, Oggy thought of a very unpleasant answer to his questions.

'A badger!' he squealed, and set off as fast as his legs would carry him along the bank. They did not carry him far, before he collided violently with the rat, who had been running head

down in the opposite direction, with the intention of helping
Oggy out of the water. They rolled over each other, away
from the water, fortunately, the rat gasping 'whasamatter?'
and the hedgehog struggling to break free. It is not an easy
matter to hold an excitable hedgehog, and the rat was con-
siderably scratched and pricked through trying to detain
Oggy long enough to get a sensible answer from him. One
fearful glance over his shoulder told the terrified animal that
the dark figure from the reed bed was already pursuing him
along the towpath. In a moment Oggy achieved the agility,
which he had thought beyond him only a few minutes before.
Leaping clear of the rat, he curled up in a ball and rolled into
the bottom of the hedge, where he lay exhausted. Whatever
happened, he could not move a step further.

The rat picked himself up from the towpath and looked
round dazedly for Oggy. Failing to see him anywhere,
he turned to the otter, who had now seated herself on the
bank.

'That's a nice thing if you like!' she said. 'You practically save a chap's life – rescue him from a watery grave and all that rubbish – and he charges off yelling blue murder. Good evening, Ratty.'

' 'Evening Miss Ottoline,' said the rat sitting down with her. 'Don't see much of you in these parts. Now, what did you say to my mate, to send him off like that?'

'I'm slumming. Seeing how the other half lives, you know.' She grinned at the rat, who made appropriate noises of protest and disgust. 'But look here, who was the water baby, and what was it all about?' she went on.

The rat scratched his head.

'Well, he's a hedgehog of my acquaintance,' he explained, 'who's come from London with us on the boat, but why he took off like that I couldn't say. Some sort of shock after falling in the water, I shouldn't wonder.'

'Must have affected his eyesight too,' Ottoline sniffed. 'He was muttering about a badger.'

The rat laughed out loud as he began to understand what had happened.

'He must have meant *you*,' he shouted.

'What!' exclaimed the otter indignantly. 'Do I look like a badger?'

'No, but Oggy's never actually seen a badger, only heard about them,' said the rat. 'He's never even *heard* about otters, so as soon as he saw a big animal he didn't recognize, he must have thought it was a hungry badger inviting him to dinner.'

'Well I'm blowed, that's a nice thing if you like!' the otter exclaimed. 'You fish a chap out of the cut, and he suspects you of wanting to serve him up with apple sauce and two veg.'

'Sh! He's very sensitive about being ignorant,' the rat whispered, in case Oggy was in earshot.

'He jolly well needs to be,' Ottoline assured him warmly.

Rat shushed the otter again and went across to the hedge,

calling Oggy. Nothing stirred, not so much as a leaf or a blade of grass, to show him where the hedgehog had hidden himself. The rat made his way gently along the hedge, calling softly, so that Oggy would not be frightened. Soon he spotted a movement under some dead leaves, and recognized Oggy, rolled up but still panting.

'It's all right me old mate,' he called cheerfully, 'you can come out. No badgers round here.'

There was no reply, and the prickly lump under the leaves stopped moving, as if Oggy were holding his breath.

'I said you can come out,' Rat repeated. 'That wasn't a badger, that was an otter; they only eat fish.'

Oggy unrolled just enough to show one beady black eye.

'How do you know?' he mumbled suspiciously.

'I know because it's a fact,' said the rat, refusing to waste time with logic. 'And anyway, I've known this particular otter for years – she's a great traveller, and a real lady. She was quite upset by the way you went off just then.'

Oggy uncurled reluctantly and crept out from under the hedge.

'I'm sorry, Rat,' he said miserably. 'I suppose you must think me terribly stupid and clumsy and rude and ungrateful and—'

'Hey!' said the rat. 'I don't think anything of the sort. I think you've just had a nasty shock that would've upset anyone. Now come and meet Miss Ottoline.'

The unhappy hedgehog trailed after the rat, back to the place where Ottoline was still sitting. He had made a complete fool of himself, he thought: through sheer clumsiness he had fallen off the bridge, and then he had to go and show himself up as an awful coward *and* insult Rat's friend all at once. However, Ottoline's first words to him changed things entirely.

'Hallo,' she said. 'I didn't know hedgehogs could swim.'

'Eh?' said Oggy, completely forgetting his manners.

'Blow me!' exclaimed the rat. 'Neither did I until just now. At least, I never saw a hedgehog swim before, nor ever heard of it either, if it comes to that.'

'Did you know you could swim?' the otter asked.

'No, Miss,' Oggy replied. 'It just happened like that when I hit the water.'

'Good Heavens!' cried the otter admiringly. 'It took me ages to learn when I was a cub. Mother had to keep chucking me in, and I kept crawling out again as soon as she turned her back, and you just drop in and swim – just like that. Wonderful!'

'Wonderful!' the rat agreed and Oggy expanded and relaxed with pleasure, not seeing the glances exchanged between the other two animals over his head.

'Well I suppose it's that I'm very adaptable,' he said modestly, and before he even knew that he had started, he was telling Ottoline all about his mother's sayings, about Belsize Park and the people in the house, about Hampstead Heath and the fox, and then of course he could explain about Fox's warning against badgers.

'But didn't Fox tell you what a badger looks like?' Ottoline asked him.

'Well, no; he only mentioned badgers just as he was going,' Oggy explained.

'Typical!' the otter snorted. 'Just trying to frighten you, I expect. That animal's too clever for his own good. He'll come to a bad end one day, and I shan't send him any flowers.'

The rat tut-tutted a bit at this, and said something about travelling animals needing to hang together a bit, but Ottoline tossed her head and blew through her whiskers impatiently.

'That's as may be,' she said, 'but that creature annoys me. The airs he gives himself: "sharing lodgings with Badger". Why if the old fellow let him use a couple of back rooms, I bet

that was as far as it went. And why should he go around
scaring harmless hedgehogs?'

Oggy was not sure that he cared for the word harmless. The
admiration Ottoline had expressed for his swimming exploit
had made him feel much more like the bold and resourceful
hedgehog again, and though he certainly had no desire to
harm anyone or anything, he did feel that the otter's last remark made him sound a bit of a milksop. He swaggered
a little.

'Oh, he didn't really scare me,' he said. 'He was quite a good
sort really.'

The other two said nothing, but they looked at him in a
way which made him remember that he had recently shown
himself to be rather less than fearless, and he shrank a little.

'I think *we* ought to tell Oggy a bit about Badger, don't
you?' said the rat quickly, before Oggy could start feeling
inferior again.

'Nothing much to tell, is there?' said Ottoline. 'He's big
and grey, and has a long black and white face. You couldn't
really mistake him for anyone else.'

'I hope I never get the chance,' Oggy said, shuddering slightly.

'I don't think you need to worry too much.' The otter smiled. 'It may be true that Badger likes a bit of hedgehog now and then, but I doubt if hedgehog is his staple diet, you know.'

'I'd rather not take any chances,' Oggy said grimly, and rat nodded sympathetically.

Ottoline was, as the rat had said, a great traveller, and Oggy was quite happy to listen to her talking about her travels all night. She confirmed his picture of the Country, but he was very puzzled when she remarked that she had recently been to the coast.

'It's where the Sea starts,' she explained.

'What's the Sea?' demanded Oggy. 'Do you go there, rat?'

'Not me,' said the rat. 'That's probably why I forgot to mention it to you. No, I'm an inland waterways man meself. The Sea is *salt* water.'

'And the whole Country is surrounded by it,' Ottoline added.

'What!' Oggy cried. 'You mean the Country is surrounded by the Sea, like London is surrounded by the Country?'

'More or less like that,' Ottoline agreed.

Oggy was amazed. It seemed to him that the World grew bigger every time he met someone new. The idea that he could ever find four people in such a vast and complicated world now seemed to him as ridiculous as it had once seemed simple, and so he abandoned the last faint hope that had stayed with him until now. It was not so sad to have to give up his people, however, as it would have been a few days ago. Then, the People were the only creatures he had ever known who had been kind to him or interested in him. Now he had met two animals who did not laugh at him, or despise him; who actually seemed to like him; who encouraged his desire to travel instead of mocking it. Sensible, helpful animals, he thought, but he had enough sense now not to imagine that there was anything special about himself to merit this attention.

'I can't think why you're so nice to me,' he said, feeling very unworthy. The rat and the otter stared at him and then at each other.

'Why shouldn't we be nice?' the rat demanded. 'Nothing wrong with you is there?'

'You wouldn't expect us to be nasty to you, would you?' said Ottoline, frowning slightly. 'What sort of animals do you think we are?'

Oggy subsided. By the end of the night, it had been decided that he would stay on the boat with the rat indefinitely.

'If you can put up with me,' said Oggy humbly.

'I'll tell you when I can't stand you any longer,' said the rat.

7 Oggy Meets Hodge

As Oggy ambled gently down the hedge which had just provided him with a good supper, he grunted to himself and blew softly, as a human might have hummed and whistled under his breath in a mood of great contentment. It was late evening of the second day of Oggy's voyage on the canal boat. The rat had gone to visit some relations who lived under the wharf by which the boats had been moored, and so Oggy went off on his own to find a meal and explore. He was now comfortably full and ready to give all his attention to enjoying the summer night. He had dined in the dry ditch on the other side of the hedge, but had just climbed out because, although he had found plenty to eat there, it was too narrow and the traffic was too heavy for a leisurely stroll. Not that the mice, shrews and voles that made up the greater part of the population of the area were a pushful sort of animal, but they were on the whole too taken up with their own affairs to concern themselves with anyone else. Having satisfied his own appetite, Oggy wanted to get away from the dull business of merely getting a living.

He made slow progress, stopping at every other step to sniff at a plant he had never seen before, or to squint at the pale, dusty moths that fluttered like dream creatures in the long grass; and all the time he was telling himself what a delightful place the Country was, and how pleasant it was to wander in it at will, and how fortunate he had been in finding such a good friend as Rat. Suddenly in the middle of all the strange new smells, which he was finding so fascinating, he

caught a breath of the most familiar smell in the world, and the next moment he was nose to nose with another hedgehog. Oggy backed a step, and the two animals stared at each other.

'Good evening,' said Oggy. It was such a long time since he had met one of his own kind, that he hardly knew what to say.

'I suppose it is,' the other hedgehog said hoarsely. 'Haven't seen you around here before,' he added abruptly.

'You wouldn't,' Oggy said, 'because I've never been here before.' He thought this was rather a witty answer, and was chuckling to himself, when another idea occurred to him. 'I say,' he said anxiously. 'I'm not trespassing on your territory, am I? I didn't catch your scent until just a second before we met.'

'Don't have any territory – or else everywhere's my territory,' said the other hedgehog. 'What's your name? I'm Hodge.'

'Oggy,' said Oggy, and the two hedgehogs eyed each other in silence again for a moment.

'You a Traveller?' Hodge demanded.

'Sort of,' said Oggy, and then, not knowing quite what Hodge meant by a 'Traveller' but feeling that his wandering habit of life needed some explaining, he started to tell the story of how he had made friends with the family in London (he was always inclined to exaggerate this friendship a bit), and how he had decided to try to follow them. At this point Hodge interrupted him. He had listened and nodded approvingly when Oggy told him about how the little girl had fed him, he had stared a little at Oggy's use of the word 'friends' in referring to his People, but now he started making impatient clicking noises with his tongue.

'Lookee here, young Oggy,' he said. 'I allow you found a nice comfy billet and it's a pity they went off and left you like that – puts a fellow out of his stride if he can't rely on getting his meals regular. But there's plenty of other humans around, you know. Any one of them good for a meal now and then.'

'Well it wasn't just the food,' Oggy said hastily, fearing that his new acquaintance would think him merely mercenary. 'They were my friends; I belonged with them, you see.' Oggy was rather proud of his Finer Feelings.

Hodge sniffed.

'Doesn't sound like they had any feelings of belonging with you,' he remarked. 'Look here lad, there aren't many about like you and me – hedgehogs with a bit of go like. Most of our tribe are a stodgy old lot. What say you come along o' me. I could show you a thing or two, what you obviously need showing, and I reckon we'd do all right together. How about it?'

Oggy hesitated. He had pretty well decided to stay with the rat on the canal boat for the rest of this trip at least, and even if he did change his mind, he did not think it would be right to go off without a word of farewell.

'Well there's Rat,' he said slowly. 'I mean I'd quite like to go with you for a bit, but I ought to have a word with Rat first. He's been very good to me – a real friend . . .'

Hodge cut in brusquely.

'Friend? You're always on about your friends, aren't you?

You really need me, you know.' He shook his head and laughed a little, then fixed a hard, button stare on Oggy. 'Get this, young 'un, a hedgehog don't have no friends, unless it's another hedgehog. What with this and that and fleas as well, there just isn't anyone who wants you around them for long. They'll patronize you for a while, try to make out it doesn't matter who you are or where you come from as long as you're a good chap, but it's all phony, see? They'll all drop you sooner or later. And as for humans – well that's a load of old rubbish. Humans aren't *anybody's* friends: they aren't even friends to each other. Everyone knows that.'

Oggy felt very hollow. In the last two days he had begun to feel quite pleased with himself. Finding someone who really seemed to like his company had built up his confidence no end. Now he felt that he had been terribly stupid, once again. Of course the rat couldn't possibly like him, and as for Ottoline, why, he must just have been a joke to her – the swimming hedgehog who didn't know the difference between an otter and a badger. Probably Rat was telling his relations about it at this very moment and laughing about him: *patronizing* him. Oggy felt hot and miserable with embarrassment.

'Well?' said Hodge, watching him closely. Oggy shook himself a little and put on a bit of bravado.

'Right!' he said. 'I'll come with you. Don't suppose old Rat will miss my company much. After all, he only gave me a lift for a night or so on the barge.'

'That didn't cost him anything, either,' Hodge added.

The next evening Hodge was evidently anxious to start early. He would not even wait for a snack when they first started out, saying that there would be plenty to eat where he was going, and there was a full moon tonight, so he wanted to be there in good time. Oggy misunderstood this reference to the moon, and supposing Hodge to mean that he did not want to travel by moonlight, he said:

'Is it dangerous to be seen round here, then?'

'No,' said Hodge grinning. 'We *want* to be seen, that's the whole point.'

He would say no more than that, and led the way at a brisk pace.

Shortly after the moon had risen they came to a very large garden, apparently on the outskirts of a town. Hodge stopped.

'Here we are,' he said.

'Where?' Oggy demanded.

Hodge looked at him, slyly, sideways.

'Well it's like this,' he said. 'This garden belongs to a very clever man – a Doctor or Professor Something-or-other . . .'

'What's that?' Oggy interrupted.

'It means he's something very clever, that's all,' Hodge told him. 'And the thing he's so clever about is animal behaviour – he likes seeing animals doing funny things, see, so we're going to make him happy tonight, and he'll feed us in return.'

'How do we do it?' said Oggy, completely mystified.

'We just go and do some behaviour for him. I usually go up to the house and snort around for a bit, so as to draw attention to myself, then I run round in circles on the lawn – that's why there has to be a good moon, see, so's he can see – and then he puts food out. That's all there is to it, but I reckon it would be even better behaviour if there's two of us. We might even pull it a couple of nights running if it's fine. It's worth a try, anyway.'

Oggy did not really believe Hodge. It sounded very unlikely to him, and he rather wanted to go in search of some supper that he would be sure of finding, instead of playing silly games. Nevertheless he did not want to upset Hodge, and so they both went up to the house and did exactly what Hodge had said. When they had been scuffling about at the back of the house for a few minutes, they heard a window being cautiously opened somewhere above them. As Hodge led

67

the way on to the moonlit lawn, Oggy heard a man's voice say:

'There you are, what did I tell you?' And a woman replied, 'But look, there's two of them! How exciting!'

How queer, Oggy thought, as he and Hodge chased each other round and round the lawn, and I always believed humans were so intelligent.

After a little while Hodge stopped and Oggy went up to him.

'O.K., that should do it,' he puffed. 'Perhaps just to round it off we could run towards the house in line.'

When they arrived at the back door, they found a substantial plateful of scraps waiting for them. A whisper of conversation came from the open window. Hodge cocked his head towards it and winked at Oggy.

The following night the same performance produced the same satisfactory results, and Oggy imagined, in his innocence, that they would now find a comfortable home for themselves in this very pleasant garden, and develop their acquaintance with the Professor further. He was very surprised, therefore, when on the third night Hodge said:

'Ready to move on?'

'Why can't we stay here?' Oggy asked him. 'I mean, get to know the people and all that.'

Hodge sighed.

'Look here,' he said. 'You were dead lucky with those people in London. Most of them wouldn't keep on producing grub like that night after night, I can tell you. They don't do it because they *like* us or anything like that – we're a novelty, an oddity, that's all. If we stay around they'll get used to us, and just won't bother with us any more. But if we go now, and show up again next time there's a full moon, they'll be on the look out for us. Besides there's more to getting a living without really trying than playing games for professors. I'm taking your education in hand, young Oggy. If I don't, I don't know who will!'

This time when Hodge stopped it was on the edge of a large field, full of cows lying like huge shapeless lumps in the turf, or moving about slowly in the moonlight, cropping the grass, as if they were reluctant to sleep on such a beautiful night.

'What do we find here?' Oggy inquired, his nose twitching after a passing slug.

'Something more interesting than slugs, I promise you,' Hodge said grinning over his shoulder at Oggy. 'Something I know you rather fancy. What do you say to milk?'

'Where?' Oggy demanded greedily, looking round for a house. 'No one lives round here surely?'

'Where do you think that milk you had in London came from?' said Hodge.

'From bottles,' Oggy replied promptly. 'I once knocked one over, and it was full of milk. Mind you, not all bottles have milk in them – I remember...'

But Hodge was evidently not interested in Oggy's reminiscences of London. 'But how do you suppose it got into the bottles?' he said.

Oggy had never even thought about it; once he had discovered that bottles standing outside houses sometimes contained milk, he had not troubled himself further with the question of where milk came from, and so he stared blankly at Hodge and shook his head.

'Well it comes from cows,' the other continued. 'Out of the cow into the bottle, out of the bottle into the saucer for a nice friendly hedgehog. Only we aren't going to wait for all that business, we're going to have milk straight from the cow tonight.'

'How?' said Oggy rather stupidly.

'Suck it,' said Hodge chuckling hoarsely. 'We're going to

trot along under some nice old cow, like two spiny little calves, and milk her for our supper.'

He turned to the field and looked around for a cow that was standing up, but Oggy still hung back.

'Isn't that stealing?' he said uneasily.

Hodge looked a bit impatient this time, but after a moment's thought, he said, 'Well now, look at it this way – it's all right to take milk that people put out for us, isn't it?'

Oggy nodded.

'And people never mind giving us milk, do they?'

Oggy shook his head.

'Right!' Hodge exclaimed triumphantly. 'What's the difference if we don't wait for it to be put in a saucer, but take it straight from the cow?'

Oggy had to admit that it seemed to be the same thing. Certainly he had to agree that it was the same milk, although he still had vague misgivings. By the time he was full of milk, he was also prepared to agree that it was a good meal very easily come by, with no apparent inconvenience to anyone, since the cows did not seem to mind. All in all, it seemed a better way of getting supper than running round on lawns. He was all the more surprised, therefore, when Hodge insisted on moving on at once.

'Not a good idea to go milking two nights running in the same place,' he said.

Oggy was suspicious again.

'I thought you said it was all right and nobody would mind,' he said.

'So it is,' Hodge assured him quickly, 'but we don't want to be greedy, do we? And country people are funny about things: superstitious, like. If any *Hi*gnerant person was to see us, they might not understand. They might think we was spoiling the milk or hurting the cow, or something.'

Oggy accepted the explanation, but he was definitely

beginning to feel uneasy about some of the activities of what Hodge called 'a Gentleman of the Roads'. The next night brought an incident which did more than make him uneasy: it positively frightened him.

They were working their way through the gardens of a village, where Hodge said there was always plenty to pick up, when a particularly strong and enticing smell of food came to their noses. Following the scent they came to the back of a small butcher's shop, and finally to a plastic sack, which proved to be full of meat scraps. It was the work of a minute for Hodge to pull the top of the sack open.

'Come on,' he said, and without waiting to see if Oggy came, he wriggled into the sack and started to eat.

Oggy was much more cautious. He pulled some bits out and ate them, but would not go right into the sack. He stood back and watched nervously as Hodge squirmed in further to get at some very tempting pieces of bacon right at the bottom. When he was full and ready to come out, however, Hodge found himself in trouble. There were in fact two sacks, one inside the other, and somehow Hodge could not find the way out. For hours he scrambled about while Oggy ran round outside trying to tell him where he was, but it was no use. Towards morning, Hodge seemed to tire and fall asleep and Oggy went off for a while to find something to eat. (He was not going to risk the sack.) It was daylight when he returned.

He was alarmed to see that someone was already moving about inside the building, and then a woman came out and dumped a box alongside the sack. She was about to turn away when a movement in the sack attracted her attention.

'Well I never!' she cried.

Oggy did not wait to see what happened next, but ran round the corner of the shop, where he hesitated. He did not like to run off and leave Hodge like this, but what else could he do? Within seconds the problem was solved for him.

Hodge, smelling most revoltingly of bacon (and that not the freshest), came strolling after him, as if nothing unusual had happened.

'That was very civil of you to wait for me, young Oggy,' he said, and led the way down the little alley beside the shop and into the field behind, at a leisurely, untroubled pace.

8 The Crow Explains About Bad Ends

After the trouble with the sack, Oggy was relieved to find that their next night's journey was to take them through a wood, well away from houses and people. He was beginning to feel that Hodge's ways of getting a living were both dishonest and dangerous, and that clever as the other hedgehog was at tricking people and scrounging meals, he might not be quite clever enough one day to get out of the trouble his cleverness got him into.

'It's a good thing for you that that woman was kind enough to let you out of the sack,' Oggy told him severely.

'Kind?' said Hodge. 'What was so kind about that? No reason why she shouldn't let me out. I knew someone would.'

'But suppose no one had seen you, and you hadn't been able to find your way out. What would have happened then?'

'I don't know,' said Hodge indifferently. 'Doesn't matter, does it? Someone *did* let me out, so why worry about what didn't happen?'

Hodge also seemed to be quite indifferent to all the things that Oggy was so careful about. He was quite convinced that all a hedgehog had to do to be perfectly safe was just to roll up and wait until the danger went away. He knew nothing at all about crossing roads; he had heard about badgers, but was sure that he would never meet one himself; he had never even heard of foxes eating hedgehogs before, and did not believe that there was any real use in being able to swim. However,

74

far from allaying Oggy's fears, this carelessness only increased them.

Hodge was joking about Oggy's caution, and saying how disappointed he was to find that an adventurous-seeming young animal like himself should turn out to be such a fusspot, as they made their way along a footpath on the outskirts of a wood late that evening. Suddenly they heard a crackle of twigs close at hand and a mutter of human voices. Oggy was not normally troubled by people at all, since most of his experiences of them had been pleasant, but something about this encounter worried him. For one thing he had not expected to see people in a wood at night; for another the voices had an unfamiliar sound about them. He turned to Hodge and found that he had already rolled up.

'Not here,' Oggy whispered urgently. 'You're in full view!'

But Hodge only grunted, and tucked his head in tighter.

Oggy hesitated a moment longer. The voices and footsteps were very near now, so that Oggy was sure they were coming along the same path. He called Hodge once more, but receiving no reply he scuttled off the path and rolled up under some thick bushes. As the footsteps came past him Oggy peeped out, to see what sort of people they were, and what would happen to Hodge.

There were two men and a dog. When they came to where Hodge was lying rolled up, they stopped. The dog sniffed around the hedgehog, and then looked at the men. One of them said something that Oggy did not understand, and bent down. Carefully he rolled Hodge on to his hand, dropped him into a bag which he was carrying slung over his shoulder, and they all moved on. Oggy peered after them, not knowing quite what to make of the scene he had just observed. The men did not look or smell like the people he had met before, but he thought that they must be interested in hedgehogs, like the Professor or the man who had taken him into the house in

London. Possibly, he thought, Hodge will now find out that you can be friends with people, and he'll stay with them, and stop going round stealing from them. He waited in the same place for a long time in case Hodge came back, but then it occurred to him that Hodge might not be able to find the way back since he had been taken away in a bag and would not have been able to see or smell where he was going. At once, Oggy set out to follow the men and the dog.

It was a very long and roundabout trail to follow, for the men and the dog seemed to have wandered all over the wood. When at last he came to the end of it, Oggy could not quite believe that he had followed it correctly after all. He had a very keen sense of smell, and did not often lose a trail, but this seemed all wrong. For a start it had not led him to a house. In fact there was not a house in sight, only some sort of old car, a lorry and a large boxy thing on wheels. Oggy finally identified this thing as some kind of house, by the smells of human living that hung round it, but there was no beautiful garden, such as he had been expecting, full of cosy corners where a hedgehog might settle down. There was nothing at all except an open space on the edge of the wood, where the earth was trampled hard and littered with all sorts of bits and pieces, which Oggy could not identify in the half-light before dawn.

Oggy shivered. He did not like the place one bit, and he could not imagine Hodge wanting to stay there. He felt, too, that the place and the people were somehow dangerous. After sniffing round quickly to see if he could pick up Hodge's scent, he hurried away into the thicker parts of the wood again.

As soon as he woke up the next evening, Oggy found himself wondering what could have become of Hodge. He felt that he must make one more attempt to find him, in case he was in trouble again, but he thought it more likely that the other hedgehog had gone off on his own. Perhaps he was just tired of Oggy's caution.

'That's another friend I've lost through being so stupid,' Oggy thought, as he crept around the place where the car and caravan had been the night before. However, there was nothing there now but a scatter of rubbish on the bare earth.

'Well that's it,' Oggy said to himself. 'He must've gone off with those men. I don't think I should like them much, but then, we often didn't agree about things, so that's no reason why he shouldn't like them.'

Oggy turned away from the clearing and went in search of supper. Although he had been very uneasy about Hodge's ideas for the best way to make a living, the other hedgehog had been quite amusing, and now that he was on his own again, Oggy missed him. He had grown used to having company and he felt lonely. Also a rather disagreeable thought was bothering him: although Hodge was so sharp, Oggy was now sure that he was a pretty bad sort of animal on the whole, whereas the barge rat, though a bit scruffy, had been not at all a bad sort, and Ottoline was definitely a good sort, as well as being, as Rat had told him, 'a real lady'. In view of all this Oggy could not help feeling that he had been very silly to give up the friendship of Rat (who was acceptable as a friend to a Real Lady), and take up with a reprobate animal like Hodge.

However, the thought that he might actually be better off without Hodge's company did not make him feel any less lonely, and he spent the rest of that night wandering round the wood feeling sorry for himself. He was not sure where to go now, since he had rather lost his sense of direction while he had been with Hodge. He woke up next afternoon in the same sorry state of mind, but it was not long before he came upon a scene which distracted him from his gloom.

Oggy was out and about early, because here in the heart of

the wood he did not think that there was any need for him to wait until dark before making a move, and so he was seeing rather more of the life of daytime animals than usual. He was particularly interested in the activities of a squirrel, who was running up and down a tree at regular intervals. At first he could not make out what she was doing, and began to think the poor creature was demented, but then he saw that she was collecting twigs. Oggy knew nothing at all about the habits of animals with whom he was not personally acquainted, and so he could only guess at the purpose of the squirrel's efforts. Since she did not eat any of the bits and pieces which she collected, he supposed that she must be building a nest, though he had thought that only birds nested at the tops of trees. He wondered idly whether all squirrels had nests in trees; or perhaps this one was as crazy as she looked, and thought she was a bird.

There were some grounds for this idea, for there seemed to be very little system in the squirrel's work. She dashed around wildly, picking up twigs, grass and pieces of moss, which she deposited at the foot of the tree. She then took some of her collection up the tree, came down again and dashed about for more. Every now and then she seemed to forget all about her nest, and stopped to take a snack or to bury something, and all the time she was muttering to herself in a high, angry little voice. Oggy was very amused, and watched her for some time, before he realized that something odd was going on. The squirrel seemed to have collected a great deal more nesting material than she had taken up the tree, and yet there was never any left at the bottom when she came down. The squirrel herself did not seem to notice anything wrong. She appeared to forget completely when she came down the tree that she had left anything behind when she went up, and so she went off to find more, but she was complaining all the time about how long the job was taking. Oggy stopped watching the squirrel, and watched the pile of twigs instead. At once he saw what was happening. A crow was sitting quietly out of sight on a low branch of another tree nearby. As soon as the squirrel had collected enough material for her purpose, and had taken a bit up her tree, the crow swooped down and took the rest, obviously for his own nest.

Oggy sniggered. He wondered whether the squirrel would realize that something underhand was going on; or would she go on taking only a fraction of what she collected up the tree, until she had managed to finish whatever she was doing up there in spite of the crow? He was not left wondering for long, for on her very next trip the squirrel discovered how she was being cheated. This time she had collected more than usual at the foot of the tree, and the crow was not able to take all of it at once. He chanced a second trip to get the rest, and was seen by the squirrel as she descended the tree. She screamed with rage, and bounded after the crow, chattering at him furiously. He was plainly not impressed, and in a minute returned to his former vantage point, chuckling wickedly to himself.

The squirrel dropped to the ground again, and sat fuming at the crow, plainly at a loss as to what she could do about him. She washed her face and scratched her ears nervously, and then, still muttering angrily under her breath, she went off to find some more twigs. This time, Oggy thought when she came back, she will take each lot straight up to her nest. To his surprise she did exactly as she had done before, although she glared at the crow, as if daring him to touch the twigs, before going off again to find more. This time she had hardly turned her back, before the crow swooped down. The squirrel was nearly beside herself with rage.

'Me bits o' sticks!' she shrieked. 'You thievin' blackamoor! Git back to yer nest afore the magpies git arter yer eggsies! I'll have 'un meself yer dirty old ruffian!'

She dropped a wisp of grass she had just picked up, and

started up the tree in which the crow was perched. At once he slipped off his branch, seized the grass and carried it away. It was all too much for Oggy. He curled up and tumbled about laughing helplessly. The squirrel ran down the tree and started scolding him fiercely.

'What business have you got, laughing at a poor old thing as is put upon by thievin' scoundrels? Up and down all day long, trying to keep the old drey patched up, when them little limbs is tearing it apart all the time. Up and down from morn to night feeding them, and their Dad nailed up on the game-keeper's fence, like enough, or run off somewhere, for he hasn't bin by us for a week or more. . . .'

'But why didn't you take each piece of stuff up the tree as you collected it?' Oggy broke in. 'Then no one could take it from you, could they?'

'That's a smart idea, I *don't* think!' snapped the squirrel. 'If I ran up there with every little bit o' twig, I'd never be through with the job.'

Oggy was completely baffled. The squirrel did not seem to be able to think of more than one thing at a time, and so she could not see that she was saving herself no time at all if everything she left by the tree was stolen. He started to try to explain this to her, but at once she flared into a rage again.

'You're no better than that mouldy old feather duster yerself. You're all tarred with the same brush, the whole lot of you – crows, hedgehogs – no wonder you can laugh, my lad! Everyone knows that hedgehogs are a dirty, thievin', disreputable lot!'

Oggy shrugged and turned away, but the squirrel ran a few steps after him.

'You're a bad lot,' she screamed, 'and you'll come to a Bad End!'

Bad End? Oggy thought, bad end of what? An end must be an end of something. He was still thinking about this, when a bird flew down in front of him. It was the crow who had been stealing the squirrel's twigs.

'What did *you* do to upset the old girl?' he croaked. 'I heard her screaming at you.'

'I laughed at her,' Oggy replied, grinning. 'She said I was no better than you and I'd come to a bad end. What did she mean by that, do you think?'

The crow laughed hoarsely.

'That all depends on who you are,' he said. 'Now for me, a Bad End might be the bad end of a gun, but for a hedgehog, it might be a ball of clay.'

Oggy frowned.

'I'm afraid I don't understand. I mean, balls don't have any kind of ends to come to, do they? I'd like to know, because

I was just thinking that maybe a friend of mine had come to a Bad End of something – he was certainly thieving and disreputable.'

'A bad end of *you*, she meant,' said the crow. 'Gypsies wrap hedgehogs up in clay and roast them to eat – that would be a bad enough end of you wouldn't it? To finish up roasted in a ball of clay?'

Oggy felt rather sick.

'Do you think that could have happened to Hodge?' he whispered.

'I don't know, do I?' said the crow. 'Where did you see him last?'

Oggy told the crow about the man who picked Hodge up, and the house on wheels to which he went. The crow shook his head.

'Yes', he said cheerfully, 'I should think your Hodge came to just that very sort of Bad End.'

The crow gave another harsh croak of laughter and flew off.

9 The Question of Badgers Again

Oggy was very upset by what the crow had told him. It had never occurred to him that humans, as well as foxes and badgers, might sometimes eat hedgehogs, and the news came as an extremely unpleasant surprise. Furthermore, he was now convinced that the squirrel had been quite right about Bad Ends. Hodge had been thieving and disreputable, and so had come to a Bad End. There could be no possible doubt about it, Oggy thought, and it worried him greatly that he had been Hodge's partner in crime, even if only for a few nights. Hodge's disappearance under such shocking circumstances was bad, but the thought that he might be heading for the same fate himself was worse, and he resolved never to steal milk or play tricks on people again.

The new anxiety did not put his other fears out of his mind, so that gypsies and balls of clay became mixed up in his imagination with hungry foxes and the unknown, terrible Badger. Altogether Oggy was having the gravest doubts about the suitability of the Country as a home for any hedgehog, even the boldest and most enterprising. Country life, indeed, struck him as being hazardous and far from restful.

Eventually, Oggy decided that his best plan would be to find the canal again. There he might meet the rat once more, which would be a bit embarrassing at first, because he would have to think up some excuse for having left the barge without warning, but if the rat were good natured enough to remain his friend, it would settle all his problems about what to do. On the other hand he might meet Ottoline, which would be less embarrassing, because she probably would not know about his sudden disappearance, but it was much less likely, he thought. The rat had been quite surprised to see her on the canal, and so it was obvious that she did not travel on it very often. But even if he met neither of his two old friends, he would at least have a better idea of where he was, and if he did at last decide that the Country was not for him, he had only to follow the canal back the way he had come, to find himself in London once again. It was also in his mind that when he had been exploring from the boat, he had found the areas round the canal pleasantly quiet and unexciting.

It turned out to be quite an undertaking. Hodge had led him all over the place in the few days they had travelled together, and Oggy's solitary wanderings in the woods, which turned out to be extensive, had confused him even more. However, he managed at last, by a combination of instinct, smell and a desire to find somewhere familiar and safe, to find his way to the canal. As it happened, it was not the main canal, on which he had travelled before, but a disused branch, and there was little likelihood of any kind of boat coming along it. But Oggy did not realize this.

For about a week Oggy lived by the canal, waiting for a barge, or a rat, or an otter to turn up and help him decide what to do next. It was pleasant enough. The place was certainly quiet, though a slight air of dereliction that hung over the area sometimes depressed him a little, and the absence of traffic on the water began to worry him. He was sure that there had always been several boats of various sorts at the places where they had tied up at nights. He would have expected to see at least one boat a day, but nothing had passed in a week. Since Oggy knew nothing about the workings of the canals, and thought that he had simply come to a different part of the same one that he had been on before, he could think of no reason for the lack of boats.

Whenever Oggy was worried about anything, he tended to worry about badgers as well, and as usual his principal worry was that, if he met one, he would not recognize it in time to save himself. He knew Fox and the gypsies, he knew what they looked like and what they smelt like, and so he could probably avoid them, if he had to, but he still knew very little about Badger. He was a big grey animal, Ottoline had said, with a black and white face, and you would not mistake him for anyone else. That was all very well as far as it went, but it hardly went far enough. It told him nothing about Badger's habits: where he lived, for instance; what times of the day or night he was out and about. It told him nothing, in fact, which would help him to avoid ever having the opportunity to mistake Badger's identity. Once or twice Oggy tried swimming again, in case he ever needed to escape by water. He did not particularly enjoy the performance, but was pleased to find that he could still do it. His satisfaction was ruined almost immediately, however, by the thought that Badger might be a water animal himself, in which case he would be able to swim much better than Oggy ever could. It was very likely, Oggy thought. Ottoline had spoken of Badger as if he were a friend of hers, so he might very well be an animal of similar habits.

'You'd better learn to climb trees, I think,' said a voice in his head. Climb trees, he thought, that was what Fox had told him to do, but whether it was meant as serious advice, or just one of Fox's sarcastic jokes, Oggy could not now remember. His confidence in everything that Fox had said to him had been shaken by the discovery that Fox did not know quite as much about the Whole World as he had made out, and Ottoline had given the impression that she did not think much of the fox at all. Still, anything was worth a try, and so Oggy started looking for something to climb.

Oggy's first attempt at tree-climbing was not impressive. His 'tree' was a small tangled bush, almost as prickly as himself, but so low to the ground that he could almost walk up it. When he had managed to worm his way into the centre of the bush, and had scrambled up as far as he could, he looked down. At once he felt terribly giddy. The ground, which he could glimpse through the leaves and twigs, seemed to be a very long way off, although it was in fact barely two feet away. Feeling that he had performed a most daring feat in hazardous conditions, he squirmed cautiously out of the bush again, and once he was safely on the ground he looked up to see where he had been.

He was immensely disappointed. It had seemed to him such a long and difficult climb, to such a dizzy height, but from the ground he could see that it was really nothing at all. Badger was a large animal, he had been told. Well, he did not know how large Ottoline meant, but if a badger were as large as a medium-sized dog, say, he could easily stand on his hind legs and pick something out of a bush like that. He would have to find something bigger.

When Oggy had found and climbed a bigger bush, how-ever, it occurred to him that Badger might possibly have a long neck, like Ottoline's, or longer perhaps, as well as being as big as – well, as quite a large dog. Oggy's mental picture of Badger, which had previously resembled something like a wolf with a striped face, now grew a long neck, so that it was now more like a small grey giraffe with a face like a zebra and enormous teeth. Oggy started to look for a bigger bush.

There was nothing very imposing in the way of trees near the canal, only a tangle of low bushes completely covering the bank in places. Oggy had to leave the immediate vicinity of the canal in order to pursue his climbing ambitions. But even when he had managed to scramble into the lower branches of a small tree, which grew in the corner of a field near the canal, he was still not satisfied, for now he said to himself: 'supposing Large means as large as a cow!' (a cow being the biggest animal he had ever seen), and the badger in his imagination grew gigantic, and sprouted fearsome horns for good measure, although no one had said anything at any time about Badger having horns. So Oggy looked about for something bigger to climb.

Oggy was really being very silly about the badger business. Certainly he had been told by Fox that badgers eat hedgehogs and could unroll them, and the otter had not denied this, so it was only prudent for Oggy to make sure that he had some other way of protecting himself than that sole reaction to danger which is automatic to most hedgehogs. But his wild imaginings about the Badger, whom he was sure he would meet any day now, were ridiculous beyond all measure. Had he been in the company of some sensible friend, like the rat, he would certainly have been told that his ideas about Badger were nonsensical. How could a monster like the one he had imagined be at large in the Country, without every creature being terrified of it? But then, if Oggy had been with some sensible friend, it is unlikely that he would have been worrying about badgers anyway.

Oggy's tree climbing kept him fully occupied for several nights in succession, and though he was always clumsy at it, and it cost him a great deal of effort to achieve comparatively little, he almost began to enjoy it. He was wandering further from the canal every night looking for taller trees which were simple enough for him to negotiate. He almost forgot the reason for this unnatural pastime, and told himself now and then that at least it was something to do while he waited for the rat's barge to show up.

The end of all this came quite unexpectedly in the early hours of one damp and chilly morning. Oggy had really excelled himself this time. He had found a large squat tree growing in the middle of a field. Its trunk was knobbly, with many cracks in the bark, so that it was possible for Oggy to scrabble up it, and on to the lowest branch, which was so broad that he could walk along it. He was higher up than he

had ever been before (though even then he was probably not more than six or seven feet off the ground), and he felt extremely pleased with himself. In the first grey light of morning he surveyed the world from his lofty perch – and suddenly he felt very peculiar. He had not been at all worried about the height when he had walked out along the branch. He had stepped out as boldly as if he had been walking along a wide footpath, but now he felt sure that the slightest movement would tumble him off. Hanging on very tightly, he tried to wriggle round, so that he could creep back to the trunk, but the branch sloped downwards from the point he had reached, and in his nervousness he only managed to slide further down towards the tip of the branch. Another attempt to turn somehow left him hanging helplessly across the branch, wondering what on earth he could do next.

Before he had thought of anything useful, a voice from the ground immediately below him said politely:

'I say, what are you, and what in the world are you doing up there?'

'I'm stuck,' Oggy bleated, cautiously trying to wriggle round once more.

'I thought you might be,' said the voice. 'But who or what are you?'

'I'm a hedgehog,' Oggy gasped as he squirmed and wriggled on the branch. He seemed unable now to get more than one paw at a time to touch it.

'Well I'll – and what the deuce is a hedgehog doing up a tree?' The voice rose a little in surprise.

'Escaping from badgers,' said Oggy, almost too busy with his efforts to turn round to answer.

'What's that?' the voice demanded sharply. 'Escaping from Badger? Why? What've you been up to, young feller! Poaching beetles or something?'

The tone and the questions made Oggy wonder suddenly

who he was talking to. Poaching? Beetles? What could that have to do with escaping from badgers? Surely anyone would know why a hedgehog would want to avoid badgers. Oggy turned his head to see who it was who stood beneath him. When he realised that he could not see over his shoulder, he tried looking down under the branch, but still he could not make out the figure below. At last, making one more effort

either to turn on the branch or to see the owner of the voice, he overbalanced completely and fell out of the tree.

He rolled up as he fell, so that his spines broke his fall, and he was only shaken up a bit. When he unrolled and looked around dazedly, he found a long black and white face bending over him.

'I was particularly interested in what you were saying,' the voice continued mildly, as if nothing untoward had happened to interrupt a perfectly normal conversation, 'because, you see, I am Badger.'

10 Badger at Home

Now that it had actually happened, now that he lay winded on the ground, looking up at a real live badger, Oggy had not the least idea of what to do. All his swimming and climbing vanished from his mind – he was not even sufficiently in possession of his senses to try rolling up. He just stared. He was so surprised that he was hardly even afraid; just numb and quite incapable of any intelligent thought, word or action.

'Yes,' said Badger, 'one can't help being interested, you know. I mean, a hedgehog up a tree is interesting in itself, though one wouldn't wish to be inquisitive, but then you said something about Badger and escaping, and one does get interested when people one doesn't know want to escape from one, you see? Or was it some other badger? I didn't think there were any others near here.'

Oggy's surprise grew. He had imagined that a badger would pounce on him and munch him up at once. He had not expected any sort of conversation, let alone one conducted in such mild, well-mannered tones. He swallowed.

'You haven't been up to anything tiresome, have you?' Badger inquired gravely. 'I can't think of anything you could have done – except disturbing my beetles – you haven't done anything like that have you?' He frowned.

'No,' squeaked Oggy.

'Well why *were* you trying to avoid me? I mean, you didn't even know me.' Badger seemed to be very puzzled and a little hurt.

Why should I want to avoid him? Oggy thought. What a
question! Who would not want to avoid being someone else's
dinner? Aloud, or at least as loudly as he could manage, he
said, 'But I thought – don't you – someone told me you eat
hedgehogs.'

'Dear me,' said Badger, as he understood the situation. 'No
wonder you were a bit bothered. Well, well, I'm very sorry
you've been put to the trouble of climbing trees, because of
an old story like that.'

'You mean—' Oggy could hardly believe it '– you mean it
wasn't true? Badgers don't unroll hedgehogs and eat them?'

'Ah, not quite,' Badger said. 'There are badgers that go in

94

for hedgehogging in a big way, used to try it myself in my younger days, but I don't personally care much for pork now. Nothing wrong with it, of course,' he added hastily, as if he thought Oggy might feel insulted by any suggestion that hedgehog was not good to eat. 'It's just that one's tastes change, I suppose, and there are easier things to get hold of – you'd have to be a bit of a sportsman to live off hedgehog exclusively, I should think. Prefer beetles myself. Plenty of them round here, you know, all sorts too. I preserve them a bit. Nice quiet coverts, you know, and a few rearing pens. Always sure of a bit of gentle sport and a good meal.'

Oggy was simply amazed. His first surprise at not being eaten was succeeded now by incredulity, as he listened to this large animal talking lovingly about his beetles. His mouth watered slightly, and he started to listen with interest, for he was rather partial to beetles himself.

' . . . and one knows that hedgehogs like beetles,' Badger was saying. 'Had young 'uns poaching in my reserves a few weeks back, so one naturally thought you might have been up to the same game.'

'Goodness, no!' Oggy said hastily. 'I had no idea you ate beetles at all. I thought all you ate was hedgehogs, and I've never heard of anyone keeping beetles like that before.'

'Ah, I got the idea from watching what humans do,' Badger explained, helping Oggy to his feet. 'They farm some animals and keep them shut in pens, you know, and others they sort of farm *loosely*, if you see what I mean. They leave them wild, but encourage them and feed them a bit, and then there's plenty for them to go and hunt. Well, I thought of farming beetles, but I couldn't quite see myself doing that: this preserving and encouraging them seemed more sporting – and less bother.' He chuckled pleasantly.

Oggy found himself becoming more fascinated by Badger every moment. He was large, but nothing like as large as

Oggy had been imagining, in fact he was probably similar in size to Ottoline, though squatter and heavier shouldered. For all his size, however, he had the mildest, pleasantest manners Oggy had met with yet, and he was plainly an extremely intelligent animal, too.

'Well now, look here, how long were you up that tree?' Badger asked.

'Oh, ages,' Oggy replied, 'and I'd already climbed another one earlier on.'

'Dear me, I am sorry,' Badger said, just as if it were entirely his fault that Oggy had felt compelled to take to the trees. 'You can't have had much time to eat.'

'No,' said Oggy dolefully, for he suddenly found that he was very hungry and it was nearly broad daylight, when he would normally have been going to bed.

'Right, you'd better come home with me,' said Badger decisively. 'There's plenty to eat there, and I know we can find a room for you.'

For a moment Oggy had dire suspicions about this invitation: perhaps Badger was going to eat him after all, and had only delayed so that he could lure him home to deal with him more easily. But at once Oggy was ashamed of this thought. He knew already that Badger was not the sort of animal to use that kind of cunning – Fox might, perhaps, but not Badger. Badger, thought Oggy, was a Gentleman, and in comparison Fox was, well, not quite a Gentleman. If Badger meant to eat you, he certainly would not pretend that he was just pleasantly passing the time of day. Looking up at the big grey animal rolling along in front of him, Oggy felt that Badger could be very dangerous, but not to anyone to whom he had offered hospitality.

Badger's home was not far off. He led the way across a field and into a wood, stopping outside a hole in a bank.

'The Sett,' he announced. 'Ancestral home of the badgers

of these parts, though I'm the only one left now. Well, well, never mind.' He sighed and led the way in.

There was a short passage and then a large chamber, from which a number of other passages led in all directions.

'This is the New Hall,' said Badger. 'The Old Hall is along that passage to the right. It's much bigger and the entrance to

it is near the top of the bank, but it hasn't been used regularly since my grandfather's time.'

Badger found a meal for the hungry hedgehog, and then led him along one of the passages to a small chamber, just about right for an animal his size. Badger sniffed at the bed of dried grass and appeared to be satisfied with it.

'Good,' he said. 'There's just one thing, if you wouldn't mind,' he went on, turning to Oggy, who nodded to show that he was willing to do anything his host might wish. 'It's just that I'd be much obliged if you could remember to air the bedding. It's just a little thing, and maybe I'm too fussy,' Badger said apologetically, 'but I do like the place to smell reasonably fresh, you know.'

Oggy agreed at once, but then a worrying thought occurred to him.

'Oh dear,' he said glumly, 'do you hate fleas, too? Hedgehogs do have rather a lot of fleas, you see . . .' He looked at Badger anxiously. His host seemed to be as embarrassed as he was himself. He's going to ask me to go away, Oggy thought sadly.

'My dear fellow,' said Badger, 'my dear chap, who doesn't have fleas, except humans and the animals who live in their houses? And parasites tend to be very specific, you know. Don't give it another thought.'

Oggy was not quite sure what Badger meant, but he understood that fleas did not worry him: he seemed to be much more worried by Oggy's concern about the matter, and went off, murmuring, 'Dear me: not at all, not at all.'

Oggy settled down in the warm, comfortable bed, and fell asleep at once.

When Oggy woke up, it took him a few minutes to remember where he was and how he came to be there, and when he had remembered it all he was amazed all over again. The thought that after weeks of dreading the very word badger, he was now a guest in Badger's home, took a little getting used to. However, his appetite soon distracted him from every other thought, and he set out to find something to eat.

The Hall was empty when he entered it, and so he made his way outside. In the passage, rather to his surprise, he nearly collided with a rabbit, who was rushing down it full tilt. The rabbit continued on its way muttering about people who didn't look where they were going, and Oggy wondered if it had lost its way and come down the wrong hole.

Badger was sitting outside the Sett, sniffing the night appreciatively.

'Good evening,' he said as Oggy emerged. 'The weather seems to have cheered up again. I thought perhaps you might like to do a bit of beetling, so I've already been round and stirred them up a bit.'

They beetled companionably round Badger's grounds, until they had both had enough, and then they settled down to talk. Oggy told Badger all about his adventures from the time he had met the people in London. Badger was deeply interested in everything. When he came to the bit about Fox, Badger chuckled.

'So it was Fox that told you I'd eat you, was it – he must have been thinking of the old days. Though to be fair, I should have probably said the same about him, if you'd met me first,' he said. 'Then I suppose you'd have learned to climb trees to get away from foxes, eh?'

'Ottoline said that he probably told me that just to frighten me,' said Oggy.

'What's that? You've met Ottoline too?' exclaimed Badger. 'Grand animal that, bit wild – never know where she'll be off to next – but really a splendid animal. She's a sort of cousin of mine, though you wouldn't think it, eh?'

Badger seemed delighted to know that Oggy had met a relation of his, especially one of whom he was obviously very fond, and it was some minutes before he stopped exclaiming over the coincidence. When Oggy came to tell him about Hodge, however, Badger seemed to be reminded of less pleasant thoughts.

'Yes,' he said frowning heavily, 'I think I know that one. Been in among my beetles if I'm not mistaken. Sorry to hear what happened to him – always a bad thing when an animal falls foul of humans, I think – but he was a bad lot from all I knew of him. If there's anything that might have tempted me . . . but I expect he was pretty tough.'

Oggy maintained a solemn silence for a few moments, and hoped that Badger did not guess that he had assisted Hodge in the latter days of his disreputable life. When he spoke again, it was to take up something Badger had said, which had puzzled him a little.

'What did you mean about "falling foul of humans"?' he said. 'Don't you like them?'

Badger considered the matter. 'I've no reason to love them,' he said grimly. 'You've only seen the better side of their character, I suppose, since only gypsies eat hedgehogs, and most other people reckon your tribe to be useful in their gardens. But even that better side is only another version of the characteristic that makes them such an infernal nuisance. The fact is, they just can't mind their own business; they're always interfering with someone else's life somehow, and every single blessed thing they do makes life uncomfortable for everyone concerned. It's not just like us making life uncomfortable for the beetles we hunt, or anything simple like that – they even make life uncomfortable for *themselves*. Now it was all right for you, because they fed you; but that was only another kind of nosiness on their part, you see – they wanted to watch you, and sort of own you.'

Oggy thought this over, and it made a kind of sense to him. Certainly roads and cars made life uncomfortable for a great many animals, as he very well knew, and when he came to think about it, all that noise and smell must be nasty even to the people themselves. He mentioned this to Badger, who agreed, and told him about how they spoiled miles of Country to build these awful roads, and stranger still, how they put terrible poisons on the plants they grew to eat.

'Why do they do things like that?' Oggy said aghast.

Badger shrugged.

'Why do they do most of the things they do? Why do they hunt animals which they don't eat, and which do them no harm? Can you think of an answer to that one?' he asked in reply.

'Are they bored, do you think?' Oggy said thoughtfully. 'I met a terribly stupid cat once, who hunted just for fun. I think she did it because she had nothing to interest her.'

'Well they create the deuce of a mess in relieving their boredom,' Badger replied bitterly. 'Tell Fox about it some time; it might make him feel happier about being chased all over the Country. (That's one of the reasons why he went to London, you know, to get away from the Hunt. He was nearly caught twice, and he thought the third time might be the last.) It's not a thought that comforts me.'

Badger was silent for a moment, and then he looked at Oggy.

'I told you that the Old Hall hasn't been used since my grandfather's time, didn't I?'

Oggy nodded and the badger looked away and went on, 'Well now I'll tell you why.'

11 Badger's Story

'The Old Hall is in a pretty decrepit state these days,' said the badger. 'The entrance is ripped wide open and the roof has partly fallen in, but all that could be seen to if anyone had the heart to use it again after what happened there.'

Badger paused and seemed to be lost in thought for a moment.

'There used to be a bunch of men round here, who were particularly fond of the practice, which they called a sport, of Badger Digging,' he went on at last. 'All that meant was that they would go round the woods with little dogs until they found a sett, then they put the dogs down the sett, and if there was a badger there, they'd dig him out and kill him with their spades, or set the dogs on to fight him.

'When my father was still hardly more than a cub, they came here. They tore open the entrance to the Old Hall and urged their dogs in, but my grandfather stood his ground, to give the sows and cubs time to escape on the other side of the Sett. He was a great badger, my grandfather; the biggest and most courageous that ever lived here, and he fought a great battle for his home and family, but in the end they murdered him on his own doorstep. When he had killed three of their dogs, they beat him to death with an iron bar.'

Oggy had nothing to say. Killing and being killed was something he took for granted, one had to eat after all, though that did not make him less fearful for his own life. But this was something terribly different that Badger was telling him now.

'I'm sorry, Oggy,' Badger said. 'I know you rather like humans, but I'm afraid you have to accept the fact that they never really like anything, not even each other. They're clever, I grant you that, and when they are good, well then some of them manage to be the finest kind of animal there is, but most of them are just vermin – you can't trust them.

'Look, you'd better know the whole truth: they fight each other as senselessly as they hunt us. *They kill each other.*'

If anyone but Badger had said it, Oggy would never have believed anything so foul of any creature. It was the worst thing he had ever heard. He remembered now that other animals had spoken slightingly of humans, or had shown surprise at his claims that he had been friends with some, but he had imagined that this was due to jealousy. He could never have imagined anything so awful, and it hurt his mind to think about it.

'But no animal kills one of its own kind, not unless it's mad!' Oggy cried.

Badger shook his head.

'Mad?' he said. 'Perhaps that's it; perhaps most human beings are mad. But whatever the reason, they destroy themselves and all other animals in their way.

'Ottoline's parents were both hunted to death as well, somewhere in the West Country, that was. I think maybe that's why she's always on the move, you know, she doesn't feel safe if she stays anywhere too long, and she always goes to places where there's no otter hunt, of course, which usually means places where there aren't many otters, so she's a lonely sort of animal.

'Ours is a great clan – the Mustelidae – but practically all our major branches are dying out these days, due to one sort of human activity or another – Otters, Badgers, Pine Martens, Polecats – all going the way of the Wolves and the Bears, who used to be the really great folk in this Country in the old days.'

Badger seemed to be sinking into a profound gloom, which was hardly surprising in view of what he had been saying. Hoping to distract him, Oggy asked him when he had come to the Sett himself.

'I was born here,' he said, 'though I've spent most of my life away from the old place. After my grandfather's death it was deserted for a while, and then his widow returned with the family, and occupied those rooms which had not been broken open during the attack of the badger diggers. When my father married, he and his wife excavated the New Hall and the galleries round it, but the family was dwindling all the time. There were gamekeepers who trapped us and farmers who shot us, never ask me why, young fellow, I've no idea what they thought we did to them. And then the young ones always tended to wander abroad for a while before settling down – often they just didn't come back. I was away for years myself – saw quite a bit of the world, one way and another. When I came back there was no one living here except an old aunt of mine, and she died ages ago. So here we are.'

He looked at Oggy's mournful face.

'No need to look so glum, young Oggy,' he said. 'I'm not sorry for myself, and I shan't thank you for being sorry for me. The place isn't empty, you know – too big for an old fellow like me to have all to himself, so I let most of it out as flats. Fox had one of my rooms for a while, but he wouldn't change his bedding regularly, the dirty beggar. Had to ask him to leave in the end – smell was something terrible. Worse than fleas, eh?'

Oggy remembered the rabbit he had met in the passage, and thought that if most of Badger's tenants were like that, they would not be much company for an animal like him.

When Oggy first accepted Badger's invitation to stay, he had not supposed that it would be for more than that one day, but the arrangement seemed to become permanent almost without either animal noticing it. Oggy found that Badger was very wise, and had indeed travelled widely in his youth, but he was also a very modest animal, and never boasted or made Oggy feel inferior. Oggy even felt sufficiently at ease with him to start to explain what an awful thing it was to be ignorant, and how humiliating it was to find that everyone he met knew more about the world than he did.

'You see, my mother only told me what *wasn't* the Whole World,' he explained. 'She didn't tell me what was.'

'I don't suppose anyone could tell you what the Whole World is,' Badger said very reasonably.

'Couldn't you?' Oggy asked, a little disappointed.

'Not me,' said Badger. 'No, you'd need some clever chap like Fox on a job like that – and then you couldn't be sure of having the full story.'

'I could be sure of *not* having the full story,' said Oggy, rather warmly. 'I found out that he didn't really know about the Whole World at all. He didn't know about canals, or other towns besides London, or the Sea. Rat and Ottoline told me all about them.'

'And of course, having found out that Fox did not know everything, you don't think that Ottoline will necessarily know everything either,' Badger said smiling at him. 'In which you're probably right. After all, she's a great traveller, and has seen this country from coast to coast, but even she can't tell you what's beyond the Sea. And then again, if you ever did meet anyone who could tell you everything, you wouldn't know whether it really was everything or not – there always might be someone who would know more.'

'You're laughing at me,' Oggy said, a little huffily, though he did not really mind too much.

'A little, perhaps,' Badger agreed, 'but I really don't think that you should mind feeling ignorant, you know, because if you thought you knew everything, you'd never be able to learn anything new, would you?'

As the season wore on and summer began to fade, it seemed that Oggy would stay with Badger in the Sett all through the winter. Badger certainly took this for granted, pointing out that it would be an admirable arrangement – he need hardly bother about feeding himself up or finding a great deal of bedding, for Badger kept his beetles going throughout the winter, and the Sett was so deep that they would never feel the frost.

'A nice cosy, dozy winter, eh?' he would say, as if he quite looked forward to it.

But towards the end of the summer something happened to make Oggy change his mind. For some time Badger had been going off on his own a great deal. He had never said that he did not want Oggy's company, he had simply waited until the hedgehog was happily engaged in some activity which would keep him busy all night, and then slipped away. One misty dawn as Oggy returned to the Sett, later than usual because he had been along the canal (as he did now and then, hoping to see Rat or Ottoline), he was very surprised to see *two* badgers sitting at the entrance. At first he thought it must be an odd trick of the light, or that he was so tired he was seeing double, but when he came nearer, he saw that it really was two badgers, his Badger and a much smaller animal. Badger seemed to be pleased and embarrassed and shy all at once.

'This is my wife,' he said proudly, pushing the little sow forward. 'Bit long in the tooth to start this sort of caper, I know – can't think why a pretty young thing like this wants an old fellow like me, eh?'

Mrs Badger giggled and pushed him gently. Oggy did not know quite what to say. The thought that Badger might find a wife had never even entered his head; the old chap had seemed such a confirmed bachelor that Oggy had supposed that the badger family in these parts was doomed to die out, but now it would gain a new lease of life. Badger was explaining it all to him.

' . . . wouldn't have been fair to bring a wife to the Sett if things were still the way they were in the bad old days, you know, but something's happened – Nature Reserve you see, whole wood protected, no guns, no dogs, no digging.'

'What's a Nature thing-you-said?' Oggy asked.

'It means, as far as one can make out, that some people round here have decided to leave all the animals in this area alone to get on with their lives in peace. I had it from a tawny owl, who heard some humans talking about it the other night. We might have them nosing around from time to time, looking at us and counting us (they're always doing something like that), but no one's going to be hurt or disturbed. What do you think of that then?'

'Well, that'll be marvellous,' Oggy said. He hesitated, and then went on, 'Will it be all right if I stay until this evening?'

'Stay until this evening?' Badger said. 'What on earth are you talking about? You're staying all winter, aren't you? Why do you want to go now? Mrs Badger won't eat you either, you know.'

'No, Badger,' Oggy said, 'you don't want a lot of other animals cluttering up the Sett now. You'll soon need all the rooms for your family.'

'Ah, but we're re-opening some of the old apartments,' Badger explained eagerly, 'and I hope to repair the Old Hall. If we need more space than that, well, there's plenty of room under this old wood for a whole city of badgers – no need to turn anyone out.'

But Oggy was quite decided. Besides his certainty that Badger would not want to be bothered with his company now, he had a feeling that the new Mrs Badger might not care to have a hedgehog around – Badger was very understanding about hedgehog fleas, but Mrs Badger might feel differently. And anyway, it would not be the same.

'No,' he said firmly, 'you won't want me around now, and I think I'd like to see if I can find Ottoline or Rat again, before I turn in for the winter.'

12 The Whole World

The next evening Oggy set out once more.

'Good luck,' said Badger, 'and if you change your mind, don't hesitate to come back here. And whatever you do, you must come back to see us in the spring.' Oggy promised that he would see them in the spring, and trundled off in the direction of the canal.

Oggy travelled slowly for several nights, sticking to the canal for the most part, but foraging in the fields alongside it. He had discovered while he was living with Badger that this section of the canal was disused, and so he was unlikely to see any barges or meet Rat, but he hoped that he might meet some other water creatures who could direct him to the main part of the canal. The narrow waterway was so quiet that often he did not wait until nightfall before starting out, and it was late one afternoon, when there was still plenty of light, that Oggy slithered down the canal bank into a field, and saw a glint of water through the trees on the far side.

Thinking that it might be another, more populous part of the canal, Oggy crossed the field, and made his way to the water's edge. It was not a canal, nor was it a pond. It was a very large expanse of water; so large in fact that Oggy, straining his short-sighted little eyes all he could, was not at all sure that he could see the far side. Oggy knew only one word for an enormous stretch of water.

'It must be the Sea!' he exclaimed in delight.

He was so pleased with the great glittering sheet of water

that he sat looking at it for a long time, and was so taken up with the idea that he had found, all by himself, the Coast and the Sea, of which Ottoline had spoken, that he did not notice the gusty wind which had risen to disturb the warm evening, nor how quickly the sky was darkening. Who would have thought it was so near? Oggy was thinking. Nobody had even hinted that the Sea was less than a week's journey away ... At last, a growing uneasiness among the birds and animals near the waterside drew Oggy's attention to the change in the atmosphere, and he looked around, wondering what was going on. A rat, hurrying through the reeds, eyed him curiously.

'Better get under cover, hedgehog,' it said. 'We're all going to be washed away in a minute.'

The rat was quite right, and Oggy hardly had time to find shelter, before the storm broke. It was fortunate that there was plenty of undergrowth along the waterside, for this made it possible for Oggy to move about a little to find food, without being exposed to the rain too often. He certainly did not feel like venturing into the open to admire his 'Sea' again until the weather improved.

The storm swept across the country all that night, and when the rain stopped next morning there was still a high wind, tearing the surface of the water into white choppy waves. Oggy did not sleep too well that day, because the ground near the water had become very damp, and it was difficult to find a dry, comfortable place to make a bed for himself. Early in the evening he made his way blearily to the water's edge again.

It was not quite such a tranquil scene as it had been when Oggy first set eyes on it. The water was still rough, the trees and bushes nearby looked tattered and much the worse for the rain and wind of the past twenty-four hours, but the greatest change was in the population, for the water seemed now to be covered with thousands of birds, all shouting and complaining to each other about something which seemed to have upset them badly.

Most of the strange birds were white and grey, with a few black heads and backs here and there. Some of them were standing on the land, and among these stood a small dark bird, who was saying nothing, but looking around with great interest. He was not like any bird Oggy had ever seen before, and the hedgehog edged towards him curiously. The bird suddenly noticed him.

'Hallo!' he said cheerfully. 'Can you tell me where this is?'

'It's the Sea,' Oggy told him promptly.

'The sea!' exclaimed the bird. 'Well how the heck did it get here? I mean, did that get blown inland last night as well?'

Oggy stared at him. The bird laughed.

'Well look,' he said, 'how did the sea get so far from the coast, eh?'

'Do you mean this isn't the Sea?' Oggy said, a great disappointment growing in him.

'No,' said the bird, 'it's a lake. How long have you been living round here thinking that this was the sea?'

'I only arrived yesterday, just before the storm,' Oggy said despondently. 'It was so big, I thought it must be the Sea. Are you sure it's not?'

'Sure I'm sure,' said the bird emphatically. 'I spend most of my life on and around the sea, and this is not it. As for big, well, it's nothing – even for a lake.'

'It must be more than a mile across,' Oggy objected.

'A mile!' The bird stared at him. 'The sea, the oceans – they're thousands of miles across.'

Oggy was completely bewildered. He shook his head and could think of nothing to say. The bird looked at him, its head on one side.

'If you don't live here,' he went on, 'where do you live?'

'Nowhere really,' Oggy replied. 'I used to live in London, but I've been travelling most of the summer.'

'So've I,' said the bird, laughing again, 'though I reckon I've come a bit further than you have. London, eh? Now that I'm in this country, I think I'll have to see London myself. Can't go home and say I've been to England, but missed all that, can I?'

'Where do you live, then?' Oggy asked.

'At sea mostly – actually on the sea,' the bird said, 'but I suppose that if I have a home anywhere, it's New Zealand.'

'Where's that, and what is it?' Oggy demanded.

'It's a country on the other side of the world,' the bird told him.

Oggy was puzzled: the explanation meant nothing to him at all.

'*A* Country?' he said. 'I thought there was only *the* Country, and what do you mean about the other side of the World?'

'Goodness gracious!' the bird exclaimed. 'How insular can you get. England isn't the Whole World you know.'

'Oh isn't it?' said Oggy crossly. 'Well I don't know what you're talking about, but unless you can tell me what *is* the Whole World, I don't want to hear any more about what isn't. See?'

'Keep your prickles on, hedgehog—' the bird began.

'My name's Oggy,' Oggy interrupted coldly.

'Okay, Oggy, pleased to meet you. I'm a petrel, and my name's Wilson. Now, what are you getting so excited about?' The petrel sounded interested and friendly, and so Oggy started to explain about how he had been finding out more about the world all summer, but never could find out about the Whole World.

'Right, let's start here,' said Wilson. 'This country is England, right?'

Oggy scratched and thought; he had never heard it put like that before, but if the petrel said so, he supposed it must be. He nodded and Wilson continued: 'And you know that England is surrounded by the Sea, right?'

Again Oggy nodded.

'Well there are lots of other countries across the Sea – hundreds or thousands of miles of sea between them.'

Oggy thought deeply about this. Hampstead Heath surrounded by London, surrounded by the country with roads and canals and other towns in it, surrounded by the Sea – but now the Sea was not just a margin of blue round the green Country, it was a vast expanse of blue, dotted all over with many green countries.

'But what about this other side business?' he asked, when he had digested the idea.

'Well, the other side of the world,' said the petrel, evidently puzzled. 'You know – Down Under, the An-tip-o-des.' He brought out the last word slowly and with relish.

'The Aunty whats?' said Oggy blankly.

'It's Latin or Greek or something for the opposite side of the earth to what you happen to be on when you say it,' Wilson explained. 'Hey!' he added, as if something had just occurred to him. 'You do know that the world is *round*, don't you?'

Oggy simply gaped. 'Round?' he repeated. He had not felt so completely ignorant for a long time.

'Yes round – like a ball, see? England – that's here – is right on the opposite side of the ball to New Zealand, where I come from.'

'Is it all birds there?' Oggy asked, adding, when the bird looked bewildered, 'Well, wouldn't other animals just fall off, if they couldn't fly – I mean if everything's upside down . . .'

'But it isn't,' Wilson said, 'it's all the right way up when you're there. Don't ask me how it works, but it does – everything just sticks on to whatever part of the world it's on.'

'Would I?' Oggy asked curiously.

'There's plenty of hedgehogs in New Zealand that seem to manage fine, so I don't see why you shouldn't,' the petrel told him. 'You thinking of emigrating then?'

Oggy was very interested.

'Are all the animals there the same as here?' he asked.

Wilson shook his head.

'Very few,' he said. 'There were none at all that were a bit like any animals here before the first English people went there. When they settled down to stay, they wanted to make the place seem a bit more like home, so they had some English birds and animals sent to them – starlings, sparrows, rabbits – and hedgehogs.'

'And they're just the same as hedgehogs here?' Oggy was delighted to hear that some people had liked hedgehogs so much that they had taken them across the sea to make a strange country seem like home (in spite of all Badger had said, he was still a little fond of humans). But he wanted to be sure they were just ordinary hedgehogs like himself, and not some special sort.

'It's funny you should say that,' the bird said, 'because they are indeed just ordinary English hedgehogs, except for one thing – they lost all their fleas on the way over. Not a hedgehog in New Zealand has a single flea, so they say.'

This was staggering news. However did it happen? Oggy wondered.

'Do you suppose the fleas got drowned in the Sea?' he suggested.

'Seeing that the hedgehogs went in the boats with the people, and didn't swim along behind, I don't think it could have been that,' said Wilson. 'Maybe it was just that the fleas didn't do so well in a different climate as the hedgehogs did.'

'I expect it's being upside down,' said Oggy thoughtfully.

The petrel was about to try once again to explain that it did not *feel* like being upside down, but Oggy was off again. 'And that really is the Whole World?' he said. 'Round, with sea and lots of countries all over it?'

'Well, yes,' said the petrel, 'a great big ball, two-thirds covered with sea – and I go anywhere, where there's sea. Don't usually see much of the land, though, except when I get blown inland and grounded by a storm like the one that brought me here. That was a so-and-so – picked me up off Ireland and dropped me here before I knew which way I was pointing.'

'It must be very beautiful – the Whole World, I mean,' Oggy said dreamily.

'It's okay,' Wilson said off-handedly, 'but the thing that really interests me is the Moon. Now what's that all about?'

Oggy gaped at the bird. The Moon? What was there to the

Moon? Just a big light in the sky at night, and then not every night.

'I mean, what is it?' the petrel was continuing. 'Why isn't it always the same shape and colour? Why does it come and go at different times? What actually *is* it? I'll tell you something else that's funny about it. I tried to fly up to it once. Flew as high as I could, until I was tired enough to drop out of the sky, but what do you think? The Moon didn't look a bit nearer than it had from sea-level.'

'I've never thought about things like that,' Oggy said humbly. 'You see, I'm very short-sighted, and I can't see the Moon very clearly – it's just a round blur to me.'

'Yes I see,' said Wilson. 'You wouldn't be able to see that it's got marks on it, then. I reckon—' He hesitated. '—I reckon it's a whole lot bigger than it looks, and much further away, you know, and I think it must be like the World.' The petrel laughed self-consciously. 'Plenty of folk I've said that to say I'm crazy, but I'm really going up there to find out one of these nights. Doesn't look as though there's sea or trees or anything, so I don't suppose it's all that exciting, but I'm going.'

'Well,' said Oggy, completely winded to discover, just at the moment when he felt that he knew all about the Whole World at last, that there was more than the Whole World to know about, 'I thought anyone who knew about the Whole World, must know everything there was to know.'

Wilson laughed again.

'I shouldn't think myself that there's any end to knowing things,' he said, 'even if I ever found out all about the Moon, there'd still be the stars, wouldn't there? There must be millions of them to know about.'

The petrel shook his feathers, preened himself for a minute, and then looked round.

'Anyway, I'm not going to the Moon tonight,' he said

cheerfully. 'I'm only interested in finding the coast again just now. Is London near the coast?'

'I think it is quite near,' Oggy said absently. 'There were often a lot of white birds like these around. They must have come from the Sea, mustn't they?'

'Good,' said the petrel. 'I might as well take a look at London while I'm in the Old Country. Might not get another chance. Which way?'

'About south-east, I should think,' Oggy told him.

Wilson took off in the direction Oggy had indicated, and the hedgehog watched him fly out of sight in the dusk.

When he was alone, Oggy sat on the bank of the lake for a long time, digesting everything the bird had told him. He thought about the flea-less hedgehogs of New Zealand. Could he lose his fleas if he went there? Fleas had been a great shame to him ever since he had discovered that people did not like them, and he would like to lose them. He wondered if it would be more difficult to stow away on a boat to New Zealand than it had been to hide on the canal boat. (He imagined a boat to New Zealand to be like a big barge, but with more people on it.)

Oggy thought too about the Whole World: the big, round World – blue and green and beautiful. He wished he could see it like that. He wished he could see the Moon better too, and the stars, which were just faint sparks to him, almost indistinguishable. He did not wish that he knew all about everything any longer. Badger thought it might be a good thing to feel ignorant, and from what the petrel had said, it seemed that one had no choice – one was bound to be ignorant about so many things, it was not worth worrying about it. At least he could tell himself that he knew more than he had when he set out; a lot more, in fact, than Fox or the cat who had thought him so stupid.

The Harvest Moon rose behind a row of poplars that stood

beside the lake: a huge golden ball drifting up the darkening sky. Straining his eyes, Oggy could just see the first star too.

When you knew all about the Whole World, there would always be the Moon, and then the stars, and then . . . what then?

13 'See You Next Spring'

It was definitely Autumn now, Oggy thought, as he trotted along the canal bank one morning, looking for a corner where he could lie up for the day. After discovering that he had not found the Coast after all, he had returned to the canal, but he was beginning to think that whether he found the rat again or not, he would soon have to be thinking about finding winter quarters. He was not ready to sleep yet, but he judged from the feel of the air this morning that it would not be long before the first frosts started to make life uncomfortable, and he would like to find somewhere before then. He did not like rushing about at the last minute.

The morning mist rose off the canal like steam, though Oggy had no doubt that the water would be very far from warm if he fell in now. The mist lay low in the meadows alongside the canal too, so that the cows looked as if they were wading in thin milk. The thought of milk made Oggy's mouth water; a nice warm drink of milk would be very welcome this morning, and he wondered if it would really matter all that much if he slipped down into the field and milked one of those cows, before he turned in for the day. He hesitated a moment, squinting down at the cows, telling himself that not one of them would mind, but at the last minute, just as he was about to slide down the bank into the field, he remembered the Bad End and swerved back to the tow-path. It was a pity, all the same.

He was so lost in his own thoughts, about milk and winter

quarters and so on, that he did not notice the animal sitting on the edge of the bank, until he was almost past the place, and a whistle of surprise startled him nearly out of his wits.

'Ottoline!' he exclaimed, peering at her in confusion. 'Where did you spring from?'

'I didn't exactly spring,' she said good-naturedly. 'I did no more than lift my head to watch a hedgehog go by – one who ought to have been looking about him a bit more I should have thought. Is Rat around?'

Oggy shook his head and, thinking that he had better explain himself at once, he launched into the tale of his meeting with Hodge, Hodge's dubious ways of getting a living, and finally the Bad End to which he supposed Hodge to have come. Ottoline listened and shook her head.

'You've got to learn to tell who your real friends are and who'll only get you into trouble, you know,' she said.

'Well, I've learned by my mistakes,' Oggy told her.

'Considering what happened to Hodge, I should say you've

been fortunate enough to learn by other people's mistakes as well,' she said, grinning.

Oggy also told Ottoline about his meeting with Badger, and how he had left when the new Mrs Badger appeared.

'I'm glad he's setting up house again properly,' Ottoline exclaimed. 'But I'm sure he really meant it when he said you could stay. He's a thoroughly decent animal, is Badger.'

'He said pretty well the same thing about you,' Oggy told her, and she seemed to be very pleased.

'Oh I say, did he really,' she mumbled. 'That was awfully good of him.' She coughed and scratched her ear awkwardly.

'What are you doing now?' Oggy asked, to give her a chance to recover from the embarrassment of being complimented.

'Going up to Scotland,' she replied, with evident relief, 'for the salmon, you know. They come up the rivers from the sea at this time of the year. It's a wonderful thing to see – those great big fish, rosy-pink and enormous, almost shouldering each other out of the water in places. Huge!' She sketched the size of a big salmon with her forepaws, and Oggy stared.

'Surely you don't catch anything as big as that?' he gasped. Ottoline laughed.

'Indeed I do not!' she said. 'When I go in among them, I'm looking for a meal, not a fight. A clout across the ear from one of those big fellows would very nearly lay me out! That kind of sport is for folk who don't have to live by it. I take the weakly, weedy specimens, that are easy to catch and wouldn't do much good anyway. That's why the humans who kill otters for fishing where *they* want to fish are being so stupid, you see. The humans want the big fish – the ones I don't bother with – so you'd think we could all fish the same water in a peaceful, friendly atmosphere, wouldn't you? But that's not good enough for them. They have to be the only ones to have anything they fancy. They can't stand even the suspicion of competition, even though they don't need those fish. Did you know that? They only want them for *sport*.'

Ottoline's tone was one of half-humorous, half-despairing exasperation. Oggy remembered what Badger had told him about her parents being killed by a Hunt, and he shook his head in sympathy.

'I didn't expect you to like them,' he said. 'You must hate them really, I suppose.'

'Not hate, exactly,' said Ottoline thoughtfully, 'I don't hate them. Some of them can be good enough in their own way, but I don't trust them. Man has pretty well resigned from the animal kingdom, you know, and become a kind of monster – more like one of his own machines, in some ways, than like any other living creature. He's got no decent instincts or inhibitions left, and just dashes around doing things senselessly – no consistency: Monday he'll slaughter half your family, Tuesday he'll save your life and nurse you like a mother, and then, Friday fortnight come Michaelmas, he'll chase you round three counties with a gang of dogs, all nearly as mad as himself. He kills for fun. I once saw Fox do something like that. He got into a pen of chickens, you see, to kill one for his supper. Tough on the chicken, but that's the way it goes, that's life. But then the stupid creatures panicked and started flapping around, and Fox got excited and snapped at them, and though he only took the one he wanted, he'd killed most of the others too, by the time he found his way out again. It seems to me that Man is acting like that most of the time. As a species, humans are just treacherous.'

'Oh dear,' said Oggy sadly. 'I know you've plenty of reasons for thinking that, but I know some of them are good and reliable.'

Much to his surprise, Ottoline said very energetically:

'And so do I! Look,' she twisted round and raised one of her hind feet, so that Oggy could see where two toes and the outer edge of the foot were missing. 'Shortly after my parents were killed, I got myself caught in a trap one night – I was very young and didn't take half enough care. I struggled to escape most of the night, and in the morning a man came. I thought he would kill me, and I was ready to tear him to pieces if I could, but he threw his coat over my head and released my foot from the trap. Then he took me to his house and kept me there until he was sure my foot was all right. Whenever I go back to that place, I wait at the bottom of his garden until I see him, then I call and he lets me in, and I stay there for a while. He never tries to keep me when I want to go. That's why I think some day I'll stay there for good. So you see, I know how good some of mankind are – some are as sane as you or I, and that man of mine is the best sort of animal you could wish to meet. But you can't always tell which are the good ones, and so it's safest to avoid all of them.'

'Well I think it's only gypsies that are dangerous to me,' said Oggy, 'and I think I know how to recognize them. Other sorts of humans, the sorts that live in houses, seem to like having hedgehogs around, clearing up the slugs and beetles in their gardens, you see. And there's always scraps as well, even without playing any of Hodge's tricks. I'm thinking of looking for winter quarters now, and I'd quite like to settle in a garden, but I haven't seen any house round here.'

'I expect you're right – humans are mostly useful to you, because you are useful to them,' said Ottoline. 'Look, if you want to find a garden for the winter, you'll have to leave the canal. No humans live very near here. But if you strike off across that field, and keep going roughly in a straight line for about two miles, you'll come to a lot of houses – a small town, actually. I expect you could find a place there.'

Oggy thanked her and said he would try that the very next night.

'I don't suppose I shall see Rat again before the winter if I do stay by the canal,' he said.

'If I see him, I'll tell him to look out for you round here next spring, shall I?' said Ottoline. 'And if you see Badger before I do, which is very likely, give him my regards – best wishes and all that. When I've seen enough of the salmon, I'll probably go and see my man, so I shan't be in these parts again before next year.'

They said good-bye and turned to go their separate ways: Oggy towards the field, Ottoline to the water.

'See you next spring!' she called as she slipped into the canal.

See you next spring, see you next spring – everyone was saying it now, Oggy thought as he started across the fields the following evening. All the swallows and house martins had twittered it to the other birds as they gathered together in the evenings a week or so ago, and now hardly any of them were to be seen. A very fat glis he had met the other day had left him with the same words. He too intended to find people, though his idea was to build a nest inside a house, not just in a garden. He had been so drowsy already that Oggy wondered whether he had managed to find somewhere before he finally dropped off to sleep. Everyone and everything was closing down now for the winter, and it was high time the resourceful hedgehog found a cosy corner for himself too.

Oggy had no difficulty in finding the town which Ottoline had told him about, but he did not settle down immediately. As he had guessed, there was plenty to eat still in the gardens, and he felt less urgency about making his final choice of a winter home, now that he knew he was in a suitable area. Feeling lazier and less thoroughly awake every night, he moved slowly from garden to garden, eating all the time, until one evening he came to one that seemed somehow familiar, though he knew perfectly well that he had never been in this place before.

He was very puzzled, and felt suddenly much more alert than he had for some nights. What was there about the place? Could it be that some animal he had once known was around somewhere? It was definitely something about the smell of the garden that he recognized, though when he came to explore it more thoroughly, he had the feeling that the shape and lay-out were familiar too. Not that he had been in this very garden before, he thought, but he definitely knew one like it, and he knew from the way he felt about this garden that he had liked the other one, wherever it had been. It was certainly a good enough reason for making this his winter home, he thought, especially since there was a very suitable hole under the roots of the hedge at the bottom of the garden. It was all very satisfactory. He wondered what the house was like.

The house was tantalizing and infuriating. In shape it was not at all like anything he could remember, but it was simply oozing sweet, familiar smells. Not just mouthwatering smells, though there were plenty of them, but *happy* smells, Oggy told himself.

He was snuffing and snorting so much in his efforts to recall the memories associated with those smells, that he was heard inside the house. The back door opened quietly, and a man came out, followed by two children. Oggy was unaware of their presence, until a boy's voice said:

'Isn't it a bit late in the year for him to be out?'

'Oh I don't know,' said the man, 'it's been pretty mild so far – we haven't had any frost yet.'

Oggy wondered what to do. He was sure they were not gypsies, so he should be safe from the Bad End. Perhaps he could try running round the lawn for them. No, on the whole he thought it would be easiest to do what was doubtless expected of him. Slowly, he rolled up, thinking, now they'll go away in a minute.

He was very surprised, therefore, to find himself being carefully picked up. He hardly had time to grow afraid, however, before he was set down once more, but now he knew that he was inside the house. There were noises of feet and things scraping, and then after a minute or two, there was the smell of food near his nose: biscuits, he thought with disbelief, chocolate biscuits, just like . . . and there was milk somewhere too. Very cautiously he unrolled. His nose had told him the truth, for there in front of him on the floor was a chocolate biscuit and a saucer of milk.

Oggy looked up and around. Four people sat on the floor round him: a man, a woman, a boy and a girl. Of course it was. How stupid of him not to have realized why all those smells had seemed so friendly and familiar. He turned to the food and ate contentedly.

'I know what he is,' the girl said excitedly. 'It's our London hedgehog, he's been looking for us ever since we left London, and now here he is. Did you see how he looked at us?'

'Don't be so stupid!' said her brother. 'How could a hedgehog come all that way, even if he knew where to come to? Even if he wanted to?'

'I don't know, but I'm sure it's him,' the girl insisted.

'Anyway, the London one was smaller,' the boy said.

'Well, he's grown up on the way – that could be it, couldn't it, Dad?'

The man scratched his head.

'I suppose it could be,' he said. 'This is certainly a full-grown boar. But I wouldn't like to say it was the same animal as the young hedgehog we saw in London. It doesn't seem very likely, but if you like to think it is, well, perhaps you could say he got restless after we left, and by a great piece of luck, found his way here. Will that satisfy you?'

The girl nodded, but the boy said, 'It doesn't satisfy me.'

Oggy looked up at them again. They did not recognize a hedgehog grin, of course, and they did not understand what he meant, when he snorted indignantly as he made for the door, after taking a look round the new kitchen.

'Luck?' he said, 'what's luck got to do with it? I always said I'd find them.'

'Shall I leave some food for him tomorrow night?' the girl said.

'You could do,' her father replied, 'but I don't suppose we'll see much more of him this year. He looks as if he's just about ready to hibernate. He's fat enough.'

'I hope he stays around here,' she said, as Oggy flopped over the doorstep.

'We'll have to look out for him next spring,' said her mother, who also liked the idea that it might be the London

hedgehog, but did not like to say so. 'Goodnight, Oggy, sleep tight this winter. See you in the spring.'

It was only when he was snugly tucked down in the hole under the hedge at the end of the garden, that something strange occurred to Oggy.

'How did she know my name?'

But he was too sleepy to think about it then.